AND HER STORY BEGAN

Ayushi Raghuwanshi

Leadstart
INKSTATE

ISBN: 978-93-5610-200-2

First published in India 2022 by Leadstart Inkstate
A brand of One Point Six Technologies Pvt. Ltd.

123, Building J2, Shram Seva Premises,
Wadala Truck Terminal,
Mumbai 400022, Maharashtra, INDIA
Phone: +91 96999 33000
Email: info@leadstartcorp.com
www.leadstartcorp.com

Disclaimer: This is a work of fiction. All the names, characters, businesses, places, events and incidents in this book are either the product of the author's imagination or used in a fictitious manner. Any resemblance to actual persons, living or dead, or actual events is purely coincidental.

Editor: Vaibhav Pathare
Cover: Supriya Balasundaram
Layouts: Kevis Tech

Contents

Acknowledgments

I would like to dedicate this book to my mother who has been supportive of all my decisions in life. I can barely imagine my life without her guidance and love, whatever I am and will be I owe it to her and then my father.

I am also grateful to my readers and my friends and family who read everything that I write and make me believe in my work. It is their love and support that I have continued writing and will continue too. It is not possible for me to mention all the names but when they would read this, they would themselves know and then smile.

My heartfelt gratitude to the entire team of Leadstart as they gave me the opportunity to reach out to more readers and lastly, I would like to thank the reader for holding this book in hand and taking it to her/his bookshelf.

Prologue

She would relentlessly write practically every night. There was something peculiar about her memoir; she did not keep her memoir in a chronological fashion which was the convention that virtually everyone followed. It was her style that was rationally or rather mindlessly founded upon the idea that whenever she would open any page, she would only want to relive the emotions and memories of that moment irrespective of which day in her life that event was being recalled.

Aanya is an Indian woman with beautiful facial features, lean and fit body, a fair complexion and brownish-black lustrous eyes and bedazzling hair that would glisten even more in the Sun. She has the height and weight of a model and is as sought-after by any man as she had been when she married her former husband, Romit.

Almost a year has passed since her separation from her husband. She could take on the world single-handedly before she had stumbled upon him but now it just seemed like an enduring and all-consuming task. She is just twenty-six years old in the prime years of her youth and beauty.

"Why don't you try modelling?" used to be the one common inquiry of all her fashion tech acquaintances in college who would be adamant to persuade her to do shows for the costumes they designed.

Though the habit of writing wasn't a part of her life before she met Romit, she found it so natural now as if it was always an inherent part of her life.

Her memoir gives an account of the passage of a year's struggle, yearning, nostalgia and the different emotions that she encounters in the aftermath of being bereaved of her beloved's companionship. Not just her struggle is what one reads through the pages of her memoir but also how she in an unanticipated manner begins to observe the several flaws in our society.

Aanya has lived her life in India, a Southeast Asian country majority of the population of which is still poor and the society under the grip of numerous social evils. She scribbles all her thoughts addressing her former husband Romit as he has only been the one closest to her heart and this is how she still feels close to him.

She had reserved the first page to encapsulate the one feeling she had clung to all the time, which now she finally fills by her last composed rhyme and that is how her story began,

> *Hasn't it been a really long day?*
> *The sunshine hasn't made its way*
> *Through the dark clouds now causing dismay*
> *Haven't I been waiting for a long while?*
> *For a morning that might just bring a smile*

And that is how most of her chapters end, in a beautiful rhyme, which is in a way ironic too as how pain can bring out beauty.

1

Homeless

"Why not visit your aunt's house for a change?" my mother said.

My mother has recently turned fifty; she looks as beautiful and young as she did in her late twenties. People often mistake her to be my elder sister. I am so fond of my mother, the perfect ideal of a mother. I can discern by the look on her face when she enters the room that she is not here to chew the fat but talk about something that is bugging her. That concern on her face evinces even if she tried hard to not show.

"No, I am better here," I said refusing the offer.

"You don't step out even a bit, not even accompany me when I ask you to. It is not good Aanya"

"It is all right, just need some time, I will eventually start working again then there will not be an option. I will go out then. What is the point of stepping out for no reason?"

"Meet your friends sometimes, you will feel good"

"Yes, I will"

I barely recall any instances of leaving the four walls of the abode since I've shifted to my parent's 'house'. I don't meet my hometown friends too and visiting relatives was never my cup of tea. Relatives are too inquisitive about what we are doing in our life. They are the ones hag-ridden the most about our well-being or rather say the ones to pass a jibe at our debacles.

My parents are not as audacious as I have been in determining my course of life. They would do only the acceptable part, what was agreeable to the relatives and the society at large. They are law-abiding citizens, law which the society has created not the government. They abide by the laws of the government too, of course.

What is the point in living a life which is subjected to confirmation to others opinions?

Is it that was life is or is it just bare minimum existence in accordance with the affirmation to others supposition.

How do they not feel suffocated? I unquestionably do and that is why I keep my distance from relatives. The less I hear from them the better.

Though love marriage hasn't been a particularly distressing issue for my parents yet my family needed me to wed an individual of their volition since they got numerous recommendations for my marriage. That's another reason I would not see anyone because I am in no condition to receive their taunts.

Cogitating the fact that people want a beauteous daughter-in-law and being Junoesque with a charming fine-looking face I did well. As far as how a son-in-law is picked, what is majorly contemplated is how much he earns?

When did our society become so superficial, Romit?

Is it the same India that has produced scholars, Yogis, Rishis and spiritual leaders that took the world by storm by their knowledge and depth of percipience of the world?

And when I call it my parents' house and not home if you noticed then there's no anomaly. For me, the home was always around you where I beamed with beatitude and felt secure. I never fathomed that home could also be a person, when I was young it was always my parents' dwelling that meant home to me.

As I ripened with age, I didn't feel that I belonged there in an all-embracing manner; no doubt it was the safest harbour where there was unconditional love showered by my parents but there was a feeling of not being whole. Not being complete?

So does it incontestably take another person to complete you? Is the philosophy which considers that a man and a woman are complete with each other true?

That is why one is even alluded to as 'the better half' in most of the cultures around the world actually right?

I am not sure of most cultures but our culture Romit, definitely considers marriage a sacrosanct union and a wife's home to be where her husband is. So accordingly I've become homeless. But that is the Indian concept and beliefs; my perception says that a home can be anything, a person, a place or just anything which makes you feel that you belong there.

You were undoubtedly the one who I could call home because that is where I found my peace and that is where I felt I belonged. I have likewise become destitute in the wake of separating away from you; I don't find that belongingness elsewhere. I felt the most secure in your arms; regardless of how harsh the days got, the inclination was that everything was okay as long as I was with you. There was no looking for harmony elsewhere or in some other thing.

I recall your words now, every one of the occasions when you would say,

"Aanya, I always find my peace with you" and that is when I would simply smile back not understanding the profundity of what it implied. I understand now that is by and large how I felt as well.

I have tried to not delve into the minor subtleties of the incidents of my days just like I never bothered you back then by filling you up with the minor details of the day but you can envision how things would be here since our parents were never truly supportive of our decision to be together.

When grief cannot find expression, it devastates the person from the inside and so in order to survive, I write and I always write to you because it has consistently been you in whom I could confide even though you may never find this journal.

I look for opportunities where there's no one around and I can have the luxury of grieving. How often I dream of myself wailing and weeping just to let the grief unleash but that merely remains something I yearn for day and night. And then I question myself,

"What is worse?"

"Having suffered a loss or having to carry it always deep in your heart being incapable of even expressing it?"

I yearn for you to come anyhow and that's when I would ask you to wrap your arms around me and let me cry because,

There is no corner in the whole house or any of its part
That can provide refuge to this broken heart
Where I can give voice to my hushed sob
And get some peace which has been robbed

2

Your Birthday

This year too there was no inconstancy about your birthday Romit and I anticipated this day from almost a month ago. The main disparity was that it was dreaded in dismay rather than it used to be earlier, filled with excitement and loaded up with energy to beat you in thinking of a better present than you would give me on my birthday.

Romit is an architect. He is as old as Aanya. Slightly taller than her, 5'10, he is an elegant man and according to his family, he could have married anyone he wanted in his community despite hankering after Aanya. They clearly were not elated and mirthful by his choice.

"The memories of the past five years played before my eyes

Without any respite,

Of each of your birthday and mine

And of how we would just compete to make the other pleased on a special day".

I always counted this day to be a blessing because it was me who was gifted with the most precious person I've ever loved and cherished such a great amount in my life. Now, look at the helplessness and haplessness that has been bestowed upon me where I cannot even hear your voice or see you on the mere pretext of a formal wish. That's something that is not expected of me by the conventional norms of this society.

Talking about the norms of this society sickens me,

"Why can't I wish you on your birthday merely in the light of the fact that we are separated now?"

It is completely forbidden as it would ruin the prospects of me having a partner again in life, which according to my family has to happen before I turn twenty-nine or thirty. This is a progressive front of society as a woman can remarry after getting separated from her husband. Earlier women were condemned to a living hell in case of separation from their husbands. It is so unbelievable to me how the widows were treated; either burnt alive or made to live a life worse than death.

Though here again you and I both know how the second marriage is, the partner chosen for the woman is and how wholeheartedly she is accepted in the new family.

There is another unspoken rule or an implicit standard about the age of marriage in society; they consider a person ineligible to marry after thirty. In most parts of India the pressure starts mounting right after one graduates and is in the early twenties. There are many sections of the society where this happens even earlier, not to mention the prevalence of child marriage even today.

Romit, you must be wondering since when did I start noticing these details and criticize these while writing my notes to you and waste the few words that I can write every night to you. To me, it does not feel anything less than personal. Everything that discommodes anyone in this society somewhere and to some extent haunts me too; after all we identify ourselves with this society. This is where we were born and this is the identity we shall carry for the rest of our lives and even after we have lived our lives.

I surmise that if every individual would leave the self-absorbed state of mind and start considering the people around as a whole big family and this society as their home, most of the social quagmire would be resolved. For one, a predicament is only that which one confronts, one does not take the societal conundrums into slightest consideration not realizing how it indirectly affects one's life in ways manifold.

Anyways it is your birthday I would want to put the kibosh on my condemnation right here. The memory of the very first birthday that I had with you even today made me chuckle and later sob as I missed that day so gravely. Do you remember that day in college? You brought a chocolate cake and a bouquet of chocolates for me. We exchanged this basic information by that time, our favourite colour, chocolates, food and all the hackneyed details which two people do when they develop doting for each other.

When your friends called me to the room in which you guys had gathered, my eyes were rolling attempting to cover each edge of the little study hall and find you and then I found you standing behind them all with your hands occupied.

In your right hand you held the bouquet of chocolates and in the left was my favourite chocolate cake. When I strolled towards you, to my surprise and everyone else's who was present in the room you got down on your knees with the bouquet in your hand and you said nothing, awkward yet lovely. People around us thought that you proposed to me that day as that is what reached my ears a few days later.

I thought that it was all a pre-planned setting but the farcical part was when later you confided in me that you never thought to do any such thing and seeing me tread towards you it all just happened, you naturally got down on your knees.

"It took so much effort to save the cake from my friends till the time you cut it" you said

And I did burst out with laughter at your face. I still remember those words on a fine evening on campus,

"Can I be honest? I did not plan to get down on my knees before you, it happened like a reflex action on seeing you"

"Are you serious or just making up?"

"Seriously"

"Ahh, we have reflex action on certain occasions and seeing a girl walk to you isn't one of those" I laughed and laughed pulling your leg over this thing.

Those days were just entranced; I was always spellbound in your presence. You were not so good at contriving anything romantic and were innocent and that's where I fell for you even more. How innocently you would tell me later that you never actually thought to get down on your knees, it just made me love you even more.

I wonder what I would have planned for you if we were together today, there hasn't been a second that passed today in which you have eluded my thoughts and amidst the dreadfulness too I am still happier than other days because it is your birthday. This is all I would have said if I were allowed the privilege of wishing you today,

Going down the memory lane
Watching the memories play
From all that we have lost and all that we could gain
We've really come a long way
It's just so overwhelming to write
Every time I shudder, I just wish you to be at my side
Such homely feeling in your presence, I can't describe
I feel safe and secure
Such that I can walk with you, blindfold
It isn't wrong when I say I believe in you more than myself
In all the moments that I had you, I couldn't ask for
anything else
I'm grateful that you had given me a place in your life
You have been my best best choice
That I'm so proud of and wish to flaunt
Alas, this is something I really want
All that I can wish today is that you find your peace
That I wish to see you thrive, to say the least

3

Fathomless

"Could we both reason out back then why we chose each other despite all the odds?"

"Do two people have rational reasons behind their willingness to be with each other?"

"Is it nothing magical and inexplicable but the logic that decides?"

I can recall that we could not persuade our parents too because we never had those rational reasons except that we deeply revelled in each other's love and companionship and you know just how feeble a ground that is when looked upon by our society.

My parents surprisingly were more considerate of my happiness and agreed to this marriage. Those who abide by the norms of the society crossed the threshold the society decided and blessed us with happiness.

I have not yet understood why love is not discerned as the foundation on which a relation could be built, why matters like caste, religion, social status, economic status and matters alike are considered above all.

I can hark back to any ordinary conversation that has so far been held before marriage has been arranged in my family and what factors are taken into consideration before concluding. Not going anywhere far away, I would recite what happened when my cousin brother's marriage was being proposed to a prospective girl,

My aunt spoke on the phone and I could overhear everything she told my mother, my mother has this habit of keeping the volume at maximum so even when she does not talk on speaker the other person's voice is clearly audible if I am in the same room. So my Aunt said,

"The girl's family isn't very well known though; you know we wanted well-known people"

"But that is alright as her education is fine, she is a dentist"

"But then my son is good-looking and the girl has average features, and skin complexion is fair, average height, not very lean not very healthy"

"Will compare the horoscopes as soon as we get the time and date of birth of the girl"

My mother replied in a more passive tone to all the remarks but vehemently supported the horoscope comparison.

My aunt blurted out all the details she could gather from the bio-data that was floated on their WhatsApp group. Can you imagine Romit? A WhatsApp group has been created where the photographs and bio-data of prospective brides and grooms is shared around with the people in the community. How can parents do that? It is like one of those WhatsApp groups where commodities are sold online. So first websites were created for this purpose and now we have reached to personal groups.

I detest this kind of culture which has been gaining ground these days. It is as if a person is being commoditized. And they call this better over two people themselves choosing their partner. And if this wasn't enough there is a price discussed between them, the price which the bride's family will have to pay on marriage. What sense did it all make? Here the bride is being given in marriage by her father as we observe 'kanyadaan' as an essential practice for marriage and the father was to pay the price as well for giving her.

Marriage today has degraded to a level which makes me feel ashamed especially in the light of the fact that I am a woman. That is the reason I have heard this statement innumerable times

'beti toh paraya dhan hoti hai'

A daughter is like a debt which the father has to repay on her marriage

I alone cannot revolutionize anything about this existent system but I feel if people like you and me are strong enough to pick our partners ourselves then all these evils would themselves be eradicated.

So by and large if we follow the conventional line then a man and a woman will be tied into a relationship that they had to carry for their lives on factors only of education, caste, family status, the external appearance and the position of their stars. I do not say these things should be overlooked but is that all needed to tie knots for life?

Why is understanding, love, respect for each other and the values that they uphold not regarded as important when these are the only things that lay strong foundation for a relationship?

"Why is love looked down upon by our society?"

This world rests on the foundation of love; it is the only thing that can win those battles which even swords cannot. The entire human race can flourish only if there is love. Love not just for one's partner, one's children or parents but love which is inclusive. Love for every living breathing creature, love for society, for the world.

"How can something so wonderful be banned as a sin if it is for someone not chosen according to the societal norms?"

There are few like us who dare to challenge the conventions and embrace what is considered taboo.

'Love can move mountains' this blindfolded us too when we were young, imbecile and so in love. I don't know how much truth this assertion holds but when I see people crossing their physical, financial, emotional limits to protect and safeguard their loved ones, making certain impossible things possible then I feel mountains are indeed small. Love is the greatest driving force for a human being. One does things in love one never thought would do. Even the pragmatists would act like fools when in love.

When I look at yesterday, look at the love and respect that we mutually shared for each other and the strength it imparted to us, I can certainly say that it had no boundaries; the depth of the emotions was fathomless.

Our love was so strong that it could in a real sense move heaven and earth, maybe it is only about the time and how things change alongside that we are not together today. I really don't know.

There's something about reminiscences, you might not understand what squarely and precisely you feel at a moment but when you recall those moments in the future you see smack-dab how you felt that time. And today I can reason out why it was always for you that I swam against the current and maybe today I can answer my parents why I chose you five years ago,

It was back then that I couldn't realize
Why everything changed every time I looked into your eyes
It is now if someone would ask me why
I would answer that it was the love that left me surprised
Fathomless! Surpassing all units that could measure its depth
Before which the deepest point of ocean would also seem to be a shred
Never did I ever witness such affection for me
It made me escape my own reality
I used to be on seventh heaven having you around
My feet would then not touch the ground
It is only now that I realize
It was the fathomless love that knew no price

4

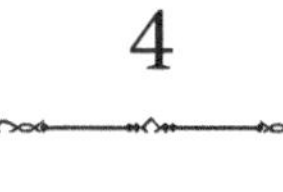

Dreary

"Can the absence of merely one person devour all the happiness out of your life?"

I wasn't a believer in such a notion or the cliché which the Bollywood hero would use in parting with his beloved. Nor were you as you would constantly quip about the romantic tales that Bollywood depicted, you certainly mocked the way love is portrayed in those movies when you asked me,

"Aanya, what happens when you are in love? You fall head over heels?"

"Does the wind start blowing or does it start pouring?"

"Nothing like that I assume" I replied

There's another interesting story behind it, the day you asked this question was when you formally proposed to me. Should I narrate the whole incident? Isn't it as weird as my birthday?

You came with a bar of Cadbury Silk chocolate which you had hidden when we were supposed to go for a walk around the campus one evening. Our campus provided every facility for the residential students and so we had a departmental store too, outside of which you texted me to meet you. I later understood why the departmental store. We sat after having strolled for a while and then you brought your hand forward with chocolate in it, which was hidden somewhere in your pocket maybe and which you craftily took out when I wasn't looking at you.

Next, you brought the chocolate before me as if it was a rose or bouquet and I don't remember your exact words all I remember is that it was a formal proposal for us to be together and your statement

"Sorry, I could not get a rose on the campus, chocolate will do I hope"

"Who proposes with a chocolate held in hands like a rose?" I said to myself

You left me speechless again with the laughter of course. That is when you asked what happens when we fall in love.

To my surprise I must concede how heavenly this earth becomes when you are in love, everything becomes wonderful.

"So the absence of one person who you loved can devour all the magic and happiness from your life?"

This struck me hard when I am myself going through a phase wherein literally all the happiness has been consumed by the void which has been left by your absence.

When we humans attach all our emotions with a single person such that he takes the place of the entire world it is then that even the platitudes of Bollywood hold true. Yes, investing all our emotions in a single person such that for us our existence seems to get defined by that single person's existence.

"And why not?"

I don't know about you Romit but because I invested all my emotions into you, my existence was around you.

Hasn't society propagated this notion when it comes to a woman's existence which defines the purpose of a woman's life to be a good wife and mother? How this society has always been male-oriented and how the existence itself of the woman has been defined in relation to men; sometimes defined as a man's wife, sometimes as a daughter, sometimes a mother.

'Ramesh kigharwali, Chiku ki amma'

As a child when I heard such references by my father's acquaintances from our ancestral village, I would laugh not understanding the gravity of the quandary that exists in this twenty-first century in mostly rural and sub-urban parts of India. A woman is not even called by her name, why do they even take the trouble of naming the daughters when they are born?

"Don't you think a woman has been forever a secondary citizen, whose purpose in life is to serve man's purpose, if not in all the cultures but almost all of them leaving behind a few exceptions?"

This society like I said is plagued with so many social evils and you'd be astounded that the majority of those serve the suppression of a woman.

Though I never had resigned to the patriarchal ideas of the society and never considered my sole purpose to be confined to being a good wife or mother or whatever these conventions would ask me to be. In fact, I never thought of marriage too but then I found you and the reflection upon life with you seemed fine.

Yet as a woman and your better half I gave my all to you solely and to be asked to feel anything in your absence is not plausible for me to consider.

Wife is the 'ardhangini' as mentioned in the Satpatha Brahmana, the man is only half and not complete without his wife. Again a woman's purpose is confined to serve a man's. But I would see it the other way round too because these religious texts were written by men which naturally implied that they wanted their own purpose to be served.

Marriage is considered a union of soul, mind and body. I would very much agree with this proposition which have been followed through ages as this is something that I have felt to the very core. We completed each other, found the wholesomeness in each other's company, united by soul, mind and body. I feel incomplete like my emotions which are incomplete too, there is only dreariness and a void left within.

Today, recalling even the happiest of our moments together would only lead me to a trance like state where I become oblivious to the present surroundings and relapse into the dreary mood. The seasons outside change, from summer's heat to the beauty of the fall to winter's frostiness everything as nature should have it. This darkness seems to have become a yearlong season that runs constantly throughout the months and days and hours and every moment.

I don't recall smiling over anything in the past few months, all I recall is that,

I would relapse into the dreary mood at any hour
Anytime when I would step into the memories bazaar
As if something would always pull me back

And I would fail to restrain the screening of flashbacks
Wouldn't you ask why it would make me gloomy rather
than happy?
Because I missed each moment's ecstasy

5

Walk Alone

"**A**anya, I don't want to say but what to hide from you? I work overnight as Zomato delivery boy to meet my theatre expenses"

Deepesh said in a low and haggard voice which did not at all seem like his utterance. He called after a year and while fondly confabulating about the college days we shifted to how things are these days. As far as I was concerned my friends would not question me a lot aware of the recent catastrophe.

"How are you doing Aanya?" was the first thing he asked.

"I am doing fine, better I guess"

"You tell me, how is the acting at the theatre-going on?

I asked ardently knowing how much he revered and enjoyed acting that he left his career as an engineer and joined the theatre in Mumbai.

"That is just great; I am learning so much here, the real acting skills. I would in a little while begin giving auditions for daily soaps and let us hope for the best" till this point he sounded like himself.

"Does Uncle still not support it? I asked and that is what triggered his agony. I thought by this time his family must have accepted the fact that his happiness lies in his passion for acting but I was mistaken.

"No, Aanya, you know I am constantly taunted by everyone in the family for going after this doltish industry. They say I have let them down so much and brought disgrace to the family. People ask my father that your son is an engineer then why isn't he working? I have detested from taking any financial help from my father. Though I don't want to say what to hide from you? I work overnight as a Zomato delivery boy to meet my theatre expenses" having said this I could feel that his voice was about to break if he went on.

"I am so proud Deepesh, I know you will pan out with success and they will be proud of you then" I interrupted before he would break. I was so moved and at the same time concerned about him that even I felt like whimpering with my eyes almost moist. He learnt acting all day and theatre and met his expenses by working as a Zomato delivery boy. Who does that when one can simply ask for money from his parents?

"I think we should plan a get together soon, it has been two years since we passed out and we haven't met since convocation" I almost took the conversation to an end to avoid any further mistakes.

"Yes, why not, we shall meet soon," he said biding adieu.

Romit, you know Deepesh well, he always had his heart in acting but due to lack of support and approval from his family he completed engineering and worked for a while but how long could he not follow what his heart yearned for?

Even during and after college he kept shooting his own videos for his YouTube channel and you see how talent is appreciated, he has a million views on his videos.

I have a couple of friends from school too who did outbrave all odds to follow their passion for acting; they are struggling every day not just because there is cut-throat competition out there in the industry but majorly because their families aren't very encouraging. Some never dared to even give a chance to their passion because their shoulders were weighed down with the responsibilities of their families and had to earn bread for their family members.

I used to be very disgruntled by our parents' lack of understanding. In India, only clerical jobs and desk jobs or jobs in medicine, law, civil services, banks etc are encouraged and creativity is killed right from the beginning. One is not allowed to follow fashion, arts, music, anything that does not guarantee regular pay checks.

But now I even understand the parents' concern, they just don't desire to see their children flounder all their life because we are all aware of the accomplishment rate in these non-conventional fields. Moreover, art does not get the much-deserved respect in our society. Artists struggle to make both ends meet and here I do not mean those artists who are well-renowned and acknowledged worldwide.

Well, what's the foremost question any relative would bombard if you belong to the age group of a school going or college going, student?

"How are your studies going on?"

This statement was no different on any occasion during all the twenty years I had spent in school and college.

Isn't that enough to disconsolate a young mind and soul to be not even asked about his well being but about how he is doing in academics? It is so disheartening to have grown up in a society where children are fostered by their parents to go for conventional jobs and styles of life. Where there is complete non-acceptance to anything unconventional. The idea which would cater to anything else than their beliefs is crushed right at its inception when a bud

Imagine a society that would only have some government employees, doctors, engineers, lawyers or maybe a few more conventional job holders. There will be no songwriters, music producers, actors, writers, poets, painters, dancers, singers, artists, models, politicians, photographers, animators, tattoo artists, jewellery designers, fashion designers, fitness trainers, sportspersons to name a few.

No songs to play, no stories to read, no paintings to hang, nothing new to wear, no poems, no jewellery, no sports? The creation of a society like this seems to be the hidden agenda of parents I assume.

With the passing years, these artists have only gained my respect for different reasons. First, we live wondrous lives because we have their works to revel in. Second, they have been through hell to defy all odds and pursue their passion. And lastly, they live for what they love and what makes them feel alive.

What a dreadful society it would be if there were no artists and no art. But that's the truth of Indian society; a child is never vouchsafed blessings or bare permission to pursue anything which is not sanctioned by the parents. Innumerable people end up getting mediocre jobs regardless of their potential and passion for something else, spending all their life doing something only for a living.

But I say do what makes you happy and your heart full. If the heart finds contentment in doing what you love and missing a meal or inability to procure a lavish one is not a problem for you then live for the art, live for your passion.

Life isn't about a bigger pay check or regular ones, it's about being alive in every moment when you breathe and that is when you do what you love.

Romit, it feels so close because there was a time when even I wanted to pursue sports but I was denied like numerous other children are denied every day. I can't blame my father as we both know the pitiable living condition of the sportsmen who have illuminated the Nation's name at international events for some time making their folks and country proud but then later sell away their medals, their pride to feed themselves and their families.

Maybe the ones who dare to walk alone have this sentiment,

With a heavy heart, I chose to walk alone
The weight withers my spirits as I am forlorn
But I know that I would learn only when left on my own
So, here I am ready to take on a journey filled with perils
With a bleeding heart, it is arduous to cross different levels
But no, I don't have anyone by my side this time
I alone have to walk the line
I alone have to walk the line

6

Fragile Heart

"Life goes on"

Not that we have only heard this hackneyed statement but we have been the ones to put it into words too not realizing its depth.

Remember that day when we received heartbreaking news.

"Romit, is that true? Anand lost his father?"

"Yes, Anand will withdraw his admission as he cannot continue this year at college."

"May his father's soul rest in peace. I don't know anything about his family; I hope things are not that bad."

"It will be alright Aanya, life goes on"

Every time we face a loss and find it hard to get over it we tell ourselves that life goes on, it does not stop at bereavement.

For Anand and his family too things went on and he joined some other college next year. Everything went back to being all right. At least on the surface for all of us, we are not aware of their struggles.

Life must go on. This is what people would enunciate whenever they would notice that you're clung to your past. Sometimes they don't realize that life isn't the same after facing a loss that can never be compensated. Conventionally, nature would have its way, the sun would still rise and set when it is supposed to, the stars would light up the sky after the sun rests in the horizon, the leaves on the trees would grow and wither then grow again, the flowers would still bloom and the rain would still soak into the ground and flow freely into streams and rivers. But our lives will be different.

There will be mornings when one would not want to wake up, days when one would find oneself paralyzed by an overwhelming surge of emotions, nights which would not pass.

Nevertheless, I tried to take up a dime a dozen advice and get along with life as it had to go on without you, but every little thing about you would make me hark back to everything we were; from your favourite ice cream to all the snacks you loved, the only type of t-shirts with the collars and short sleeves you loved to wear, the games you'd play on your mobile phone even after graduating from college, the music that you played, the marvel movies and just anything and everything. My heart would then sink and I would be lost again oblivious to my present surroundings.

At times, I couldn't avoid things that reminded me of you, firstly because I couldn't practically even do that and secondly because maybe a part of me always looked for you in everything that I found around.

What a battle it is that I fight every day of consciously not wanting to think of you and unconsciously wanting to think only about you

Though I have nearly confined myself to the four walls of the house there are evenings when I would go for a walk on the terrace to remind myself how beautiful the sunsets still are and how soothing the wind is which would touch my body and leave making me feel alive.

And then sometimes I catch the sight of Sharma Uncle who lives right next to our house. He is an old man, a sexagenarian with an almost bald scalp, a very lean figure as if malnourished. He lives all alone; he has no family as he was never married. In the evenings I mostly see him washing his uniform dutifully with great effort. He is a watchman and an honest bread earner. My heart fills with sympathy and love for this old man.

I wonder if I would be in a similar state when I grow old. All alone with only my work and my empty house. Will someone then look at me with sympathy in his eyes the way I look at Sharma Uncle?

Romit, you just knew how it was a part of my daily ritual to visit the terrace on the evenings and not miss a sunset if given the chance to watch it. The orange hue of the sky was peaceful in a sense I cannot define through words. How the sun's colour would change to dark red like the crimson powder a woman wears on her head after marriage.

Now the emotions are different and everything that I used to feel once watching the sunsets is also different.

It's just startling how a thing as plain as a song can make all the memories rush back in seconds? A thousand memories start playing without any pause right before our eyes, how a wave of nostalgia runs through the body leaving Goosebumps on the skin and a raised heartbeat. Something of that sort happened today when I played one of the many songs to which our memories were attached. I had long abstained from doing that anticipating that I would not be able to bear the sound of it being played in your absence. I had long abstained from doing anything we did together or coming across anything that you loved.

The human heart is very fragile I say,

> *It being just another evening on a monsoon day*
> *Sun had set an hour ago letting darkness in*
> *With the disappearance of the last ray*
> *I couldn't take my eyes off the beautiful trees*
> *Shadowing the yellowish lights on the street*
> *I felt the wind, it was damp and cold*
> *Left goose bumps on my skin, as I strolled*
> *I was high and left unconsoled*
> *Immersed in poetry and music that narrated stories untold*
> *Next an array of memories flashed before my eyes*
> *As I accidentally played a song which took me by surprise*
> *When they say human heart is very fragile*
> *It can shatter by the simplest of things like a song, they are right*
> *So I was even more intoxicated by the words it played*
> *Couldn't get past over it until the next morning ray*

7

Fighting Every Day

"Romit, people always say that time is a great healer but, in my case, it just does not seem to work".

I told you on several occasions when we dwelled together.

Maybe the universal rules are not as universal as they claim to be. Maybe it just works in a disparate manner for every individual. Not everything works for everyone.

I was only seven when my grandfather passed away and that age would not allow me to comprehend the reasons which took him away. He died of pancreatic cancer. Time heals everything but in the case of cancer, time takes everything away. Life slips away right before our eyes. No matter how much we fight, it slips away as if we are trying to hold sand in our hands which ultimately has to slip no matter how hard we try to hold it together.

I dread cancer as it first devours the spirit and then the body of the person. A slow and painful death, no one deserves that.

As the days get ahead, it has started getting all the harder to make peace with the fact that the rest of my life has to pass devoid of your company.

I try to keep my chin up before my family as that's the least I can do. I wonder how you have been carrying on with life since I left, do you too fight everyday like me without any sigh? You have now moved to a distant land, a different country with different people, different cultures, no familiar faces, nothing to remind you of your past years. This is something you never intended to do. It was never a part of your plan to leave this country and your family.

"I am leaving India," you told me on the only call I received from you after separation.

"The flight is tomorrow" you added after a brief pause when I could not say a word.

"Just take care there" I managed to say as I could not say anything else.

Well, leastways you called and informed me. I was glad.

I can still hear these words so loud and clear if I want to, those words sent a chilling wave through my body, I could feel the Goosebumps, it was as if everything was brought to a standstill and I was paralyzed at that moment, unable to utter a single word, no reaction, nothing at all. I could not say anything else to you and after waiting for a few seconds you hung up.

I still picture that day and that last time I heard your voice and try to think as to what I would have said if I wasn't paralyzed.

"Please stay?"

"Will I never get to see you again?"

"Take me along?"

What exactly would have stopped you from leaving, I do not know. Then I think maybe it is for the best that I could not speak at all because my voice would have broken and that is the last thing I would have wanted.

Romit left India a few months ago which was also a few months after separation from Aanya. They both graduated from the same college studying architecture for five years, were together for six years before finally saying goodbye. Romit proposed Aanya at the end of the first year. They would spend all time together from dawn till dusk, having every meal of the day together beginning from breakfast till dinner and the common ice cream they liked at any time of the day.

The first four years of togetherness were just blissful, growing in each other's company and facing the highs and lows of their relationship together. After completing graduation, they told their families about each other. That's where the problems started to rise. Although at last, they married each other that was much to the disappointment of Romit's family. After two years of being married, they finally separated.

Romit now works for an international group that is based in Canada. Apart from the last call telling her about his departure there had been no communication between them before that call and there was none after it.

Though I am oblivious to the conditions there around you I know you have always been stronger than the two of us and also one of the strongest people I have known who would take on anything without any sigh.

How fondly I had always looked upon you whenever I needed strength. Do you remember each time I feared taking on a new endeavour I would always ask you to be there, to remind me that you are always here and that would provide me with the much-needed strength. I reposed just everything in you.

Before the time that we had met and became an important part of each other's life, things were not the same. That was the time when I would stand strong and take on the world single-handedly; I never felt the need to hear anyone's assurance about anything. How did it then change? Earlier, I never knew what it was like to have someone on your side no matter how rough the road got and after having you I met comfort and security. I realized just how reassuring can someone's words be. I got used to the comfort you provided that I forgot how I could deal with the potholes that lay ahead in my way.

That is precisely one of the reasons why it is harder for me to walk this rough road this time. Having been accustomed to the shade that was always there whenever I would step outside in the scorching sun, now that it has been taken away, I am not prepared to deal with the heat on my own.

Nevertheless, I am trying my best because that is what you would have wanted me to do, I sometimes imagine you saying the words which you would have said on seeing me struggling and I just want to let you know that I am,

> *Keeping up the fight every day*
> *With every moment of the clock ticking away*
> *Relentless efforts to keep bleakness at bay*
> *Yes, I'm fighting every single day*
> *To have the odds in my favour*
> *And show that I'm braver*
> *That I'm just another wayfarer*
> *Stupefied by life and its different flavours*

I'm treading along the different ways
Trying to be stronger than yesterday
Yes I'm fighting every single day

8

Words, All Haywire

"I do feel like butterflies in my stomach when I see you or hear your voice"

"Has the earth become heaven with you that everything is so beautiful all of a sudden?"

Do you remember the first time that I wrote something? These were the words I used precisely in one of the first write-ups wherein I expressed my emotions, my feelings for you.

That was when I had to express how I felt being around you, almost five years ago and when I showed it to you all you said was

"Aanya, oh God, you can write just about anything!"

I was an inexpressive person, even if I felt things I would fail to express, the words were always plain even though I might be overly joyful or excited about anything. It was some disability, I guess. Disability to express how you feel; Have you ever given a thought to how heavy this burden can weigh on one's heart, the burden that he cannot express himself. The emotions get repressed all the time and add to the weight and someday the weight becomes too heavy for the heart to carry.

I, fortunately, got the hang of expressing myself better with written words but that was only after you entered my life. Your presence made me feel the intensity of emotions which I had never felt. I learnt not just about love but I began understanding every other beautiful emotion like humility, kindness, compassion, selflessness, sacrifice and every other emotion the depth of which I never felt until I learnt how to love.

You were the reason I learned to rhyme and express the love that we embraced. I still wonder if it was not for you, I would have never written about anything and would have been the same inexpressive person sans emotions sans the ability to feel.

How beautiful are the changes that love brings about in a person's life, it makes him a completely different person. This has so far been true for both of us as love changed us wholly. I was a different person before having met you and the change has just been beautiful. It made me appreciate life, made me feel that there can be avariciousness for life, that life isn't merely existence but it is a beautiful feeling to be lived through.

Maybe love even makes you healthy as you are content on the inside and that is perhaps why my health seems to be failing.

I just have trouble eating food because of the low appetite and bloating in my abdomen. That makes my body weak.

I hope that you have been eating fine Romit. Now that you are in a foreign land food must be different but I hope you must be relishing in sundry delights. But you being a vegetarian might find it a little difficult to adjust but you will do. You can cook for yourself too, oh how did I forget? How your Bhindi Masala won my heart.

"Aanya I have brought lunch for you today"

"What in lunch?"

"Your favourite one"

"Umm, don't tell me, is it Bhindi?"

"Yes"

That was when we were in the first year of college and you did not stay in the college campus and stayed in the city. You told me that you knew cooking.

"Did you only cook it?"

"Umm, yes, is it bad? I tasted before keeping it."

"When did you cook it? You have to hop on the bus in the morning at 7!"

"I just did, you have to finish it all"

I particularly asked about the time because our friend would not stop pulling my leg saying,

"Romit woke up at 4 in the morning to cook for you"

Those initial days I was still not a person to feel emotions at a depth. If I was the person I am today, my eyes would have welled up with tears of joy and gratefulness because I feel everything deeply now. It wasn't the same back then.

Then that year there were many days when you brought food which you cooked yourself. It was very hard for you to save it from your friends you would always say and thus avoided bringing any on most days.

I believe those acts of yours, those acts which may seem to be simple but they meant the world to me and helped me transform. It was as if I learnt to feel because of you. Gradually you made me believe in love. And steadily I fell for you.

Romit before I met you, my words were all haywire and then you were the one to put them in order, in a beautiful rhyme. Such was the effect of your presence in my life. I couldn't even express anything as I did after you entered my life.

Whenever I think of that time, this is what rings in my mind,

My words were all haywire
Before you arrived and became my utmost desire
These words knew nothing about rhythm
You entered the verses and synchronized all of them
How to my thoughts, you gave a voice
Not just once, twice or thrice
But innumerable times
You taught me this beautiful expression of love
Which is a blessing sent from above?
You then became my need somehow
Loosing which I just could not allow
I miss you not being around
And my verses seem to lack that melodious sound

9

Moments of Luxury

"How revisiting the most beautiful memories can sometimes be the most painful"

It was the first year of college, I had some issues with our college therefore some seniors suggested to me that migration was an alternative way out in the second year. They told me about the colleges I could migrate to among which I preferred the one in Pune. I don't know I just wanted to move to that city, it drew me towards it. The lush green Sahyadri ranges beckoned me. More than the institution it was the place that appealed to me.

It was a lucrative offer too, from the noisy polluted Delhi to a more calm and serene Pune with those lavish mountains around the city. I could also escape the frosty and smoggy winters and scorching heat of the summers.

"Aanya, are you seriously planning to move next year?" you asked after having heard it around from someone.

"I don't know for sure, what do you suggest?"

"Just let me know if that is your plan, I will apply too"

"What? Romit? But why would you do that?" I was startled though there was a broad smile on my face which I could not help.

"I want to be where you are," you said which was indirectly suggesting that we could be together

"Okay" After that day I never thought about migration again. I gave up that lucrative offer for your company.

It has been years since that conversation, I don't know if you might be able to recall or not but these memories are my priceless possessions. How it was all so succinct, we exchanged only a few words and said a lot.

Our body performs certain functions involuntarily, without our permission. Like these days when I revisit our memories my heart sinks and eyes turn moist, at times these eyes get over flooded with tears being so rebellious, not caring a bit of my command to stop.

These eyes were so rebellious even that day when the idea of parting was first proposed by you. I too said irately though with a broken voice,

"Do what you feel is right!"

Anyways, you know what bothers me more? the fact of not being able to even lament over my loss. Privacy seems to be an alien concept when it comes to Indian families with little exception of the upper class who are a handful of the billion population of India.

We often look for privacy to lament because this world does not expect us to be weak. We always cry to the pillow at night before going to sleep when there is no one around to hear the hushed sobs or witness our moist, red swollen eyes.

They say, laugh and the world laughs with you, weep and you weep alone.

I wonder why isn't there an acceptance to all the emotions that make up a human being. It is not just happiness or joy or other positive emotions only that a human feels but also pain and sorrow which are an inevitable part of being a human. A human is complete only when he can feel all the emotions entirely and not just a few hand-picked positive ones.

Why wouldn't people let the other express his grief at times when he is weak? Our society is fundamentally flawed in just so many ways and on the emotional front, it is flawed devastatingly. Most people do not even know that there is any such thing as emotional well-being. The suppression of these negative emotions destroys the inner well being of a person, his fundamental structure, his mental state.

I have a lot of complaints about how things are dealt with, in this society, but being a part of it, sometimes I am compelled to abide by the rules that have been framed. Alas, I can't even express how vulnerable I am these days, emotionally traumatized to the extent that a mild rebuke from a stranger can make me wail like a baby.

I often look for moments of privacy when I can be free to be weak but rarely manage to find some. Whenever at home, I am surrounded by my parents whose constant vigilance to make sure that I'm doing fine keeps me watchful of their steps to my room at any hour of the day.

We both are not ignorant of the condition out of the house, the land is so densely inhabited that we do not need any detectives for surveillance like other countries with scanty populations do; our neighbours can do the job just fine. So venturing out in the hope to find seclusion runs out of option.

My ultimate escape is when everyone in the house sleeps and then I can cry for hours undisturbed, unbothered and uncaring that someone might look at my face and then catch me red-handed or rather say red-eyed or red-faced? Ha-ha, see how all this has already messed with my fundamental structure that I am making such lame jokes.

Even at night, I can't afford to make any sound, anything that might wake my parents up and bring them to my room taking away my moments of luxury.

"Luxury?"

"Is lamenting a luxury?"

Yes, indeed it is, only a few are privileged to lament, who can just sit all day, take a break from life, take no notice of what's happening outside because they can afford to. A few days off their normal life wouldn't affect them. But then there are people who have to labour everyday to pay for each meal every single day. I don't just mean the daily wage workers but also every common man or woman who cannot stop working or taking care of his family because they just cannot afford to. Life is harsh for them.

You know how middle-class families like ours have a small house which is comfortably large to accommodate the family members but not sufficient to offer any privacy. It gets worse in winters with no fans, coolers or air conditioners working and the air being eerie quiet, so quiet that even the ticking of the clocks is audible effortlessly.

I can never actually find my way out of this dilemma but I get fortunate at times when no one except me stays in the

house. Though they make sure that it doesn't happen often
bearing in mind my general depressed state but yet whenever
I have the luxury of those moments,

> *I often would submit to unrestrained flow of thoughts*
> *Which would then take me to that time, years back?*
> *And after having those pictures rewind*
> *I would give myself the luxury of weeping unconfined*
> *In the moments of solitude*
> *Which were though rare, I managed to gather few*
> *These moments of luxury were far too precious*
> *As I would drown in the ocean of remembrance*
> *Of every single moment of those shadowy days*
> *When my heart was set ablaze*

10

Watch Sunsets at Dusk

Whenever I had to count my happy hours, the ones spent with you undoubtedly topped the list. Do you remember once when you asked me before a weekend during college years?

"So, do you want to go anywhere Aanya?"

"Somewhere close to nature and peace, more of calmness and less of people? Any historic place, shall we visit? Even those places are peaceful and mostly abound in nature."

"What do those places have to offer? There is nothing worth visiting those spots, those places are presumably haunted!"

"Romit, you know I like to explore such places either historic or some natural spot"

"I would suggest let's go to some good place to eat, what is more, heavenly on this planet than food?"

"No, I don't want to just stuff myself up with food, I will go where I want to, you are most welcome to join"

"Alright then, enjoy!"

We ended up with disagreement and at last, you went to someplace to eat and I with a few more friends visited Qutub Minar that weekend. We had so many places to explore in and around Delhi during our college years but our different choice always led to such arguments and we rarely have visited any monument together. I sure accompanied you at times to all the food hubs in the city but you would never accompany me. You loved the food so much, that's probably why you cooked too and that too delicious finger-licking food. Not every woman gets a partner who can cook, I always felt fortunate for this skill of yours.

I've always been fond of spending as much time as I could in the lap of nature. So we would always plan our little vacations to places that would fit these criteria. So when I had to count my happy hours then the hours of the dusk when I would watch the sunset on the horizon far away coupled with the soothing wind which was never very cold or harsh in any season of the year always made it to the list, such peace the orange hue of the sky along with the last reddish rays would give me.

This is not a recent habit that I have developed but one which I have been following since years, being a nature lover I never loved spending time before screens and always preferred my own company amidst nature. And you would say,

"Are you sure you want to miss this movie?"

"Yes, I would rather sit outside"

Not just you, people who be more surprised when I would say,

"I just sit idle at times under the open sky at evenings"

I went a step farther not being reluctant to call it my hobby. But you see just how different things can get, the feelings can change entirely, the perception reversed with time as we go through different life-changing experiences.

Sadly, there also has been a drastic change in the feeling associated with watching these sunsets. Instead of filling me with peace these hours remind me of the emptiness inside and make me want to enclose myself in some cocoon as if this external layer would somehow stop the feeling of emptiness inside.

I do not know why but I feel like enclosing myself to avoid every aspect of the external world. I wish to sleep inside the cocoon and not feel anything for a while maybe to metamorphose into a stronger version of myself who would again be avaricious for life.

Sunsets mark the end of the day. Is my endearment for sunsets wrong? People in our Hindu community say that one must witness the sunrise and not sunset. Sunrise signifies beginning and sunset signifies the end. But I have for eternity found sunsets so alluring, I reject their propositions totally.

There is this feeling though that this is it, as if there is no tomorrow. Or maybe just some more time. But I have my entire life before me, isn't it? I am only twenty-six.

We, ordinary humans, are fallible and frail by nature; even when we are aware of the unfeasibility of something, we go on demanding the same not wanting to accept the truth.

'Clinging between hope and utter disappointment'

Each day I try to find the same calm that I used to earlier but instead it makes me want you even more, maybe because

I dreamt of spending all my life's sunsets along with you. This is what I do when I watch the sun setting in the evening hours of the day, my heart keeps yearning for you and this is all it says,

> *I just want you to be here by my side*
> *Allowing me to hear your assuring voice*
> *While you would just hold me tight*
> *Never let me go out of your sight*
> *In these beautiful hours approaching dusk*
> *The time when I am scared the most*
> *Of being alone, without you*
> *My heart sinks when it demands you*
> *I don't feel safe anywhere except when you are around*
> *World seems a better place and I feel sound*
> *If my prayers would one day somehow work*
> *We would spend each day together and watch sunsets at dusk*
> *Till then hope would be my only aid*
> *To survive these days before I fade*

11

Happiness Forever

"Why would you watch these movies that would make you weep?"

"Romit, I never pick the ones that would make me weep but the ones that would touch me and touch me deeply, now these tears only imply that I've been moved and that is a healthy state of mind for a human to be empathetic and feel things"

"Watch Marvels"

(Me bursting out of laughter)

"And what do you see in those superhero movies from the comics meant for little kids?"

"What are you talking about? Adults around the world are marvel fans"

"But there is no denying the fact that it is a comic creation, comics, meant to serve the children's purpose"

"Watch whatever you want, just don't make me watch that with you and I won't force you too, Deal?"

"Deal"

There always used to be a clash of interest between us both when we had to watch a movie together because of the different yardsticks we would keep to pick any title. Where my touchstone was always restricted to a deep thought-provoking and touching movie, you would always want light humour, action and science fiction.

Alas, we would just not watch many together. We were wise enough to respect each other's choice and why to inflict torture over the other for two-three hours. Ha-ha, again some internal turbulence making me crack a bad joke.

Most of us lean towards watching or reading stories that always have a happy end. Even though those are merely stories, a manifestation of one's imagination but yet we associate our emotions to the stories and the characters in the stories. We start identifying that character with us even if for a while, we experience everything that the character goes through and hence very rationally we prefer a happy end. If the end is not happy then we feel that we are left unsatisfied and betrayed.

Anticipation of a happy end is then human nature as we already have developed empathy for the characters in the story. We are equally moved as the fictional story unfolds as if it is a real-life event.

Likewise, the stories which end tragically are irksome in some way because we tend to seek happiness and satisfaction even if it comes after numerous struggles at the end of the day. Most of the storywriters, play writers, novelists would anyhow try to bring a happy end to the story after the peaks and valleys so that at the end the reader goes home with contentment.

Everyone too desires that their own story be a happy one and so was my heart's only desire to see us happy together in the long run. Now if our story is written, it wouldn't find many readers because it ended abruptly and sadly! Whatsoever may the reasons be, the readers would never find satisfaction on reading our story which is not 'happily ever after'.

The happiness on the face of the bride who is going to marry the love of her life or on that woman's face who is being proposed by the one she loves is unmatched. Anyone can tell by a mere glance of their faces how unbound happiness has been showered on them. Similar was my fairy-tale when you proposed, those days the face would gleam with a different glow. Only those could tell the secret behind the glow who themselves had loved someone in their life.

I felt in that moment that the story was already written. I could picture all the years of life ahead with certainty for there was only one thing till that day I was so sure about and that was us.

'But life is both high and low

Alike a wave which has both crest and trough'

I never thought our story would ever turn out be a tragedy and even today I cannot accept that it has happened.

One lives in denial when one cannot accept the truth; it shows that one is not strong enough to let that sink in. I have almost been living in denial since then because I am not that strong.

You certainly were always so strong.

"You look cute" when I first said when we were just getting to know each other, your reaction was hilarious.

"You can abuse me but don't call me cute!" You said scornfully, so offended.

I wondered and laughed at the same time; I couldn't decipher your thoughts. Why would someone hate this compliment? Is that because he is a guy? So now even compliments were gender classified?

You always portrayed a tough exterior and thus anyone calling you cute wasn't tolerable to you. And that is where I found the ultimate weapon to tease you; all I had to do was say that you look cute and the look on your face was as if someone stole all your property and ran away hurling abuses at you.

I would have been the most fortunate person if that happiness would have lasted for our lifetime. There is nothing that can ever stand anywhere close to the sanctity and blissfulness that true love harbours. Maybe I am still fortunate than many who haven't experienced the heavenly bliss of being loved, if not for a lifetime the few years have given me the memories to cherish forever as,

I couldn't have known what home meant
Couldn't have known that love was sacrosanct
Couldn't have deciphered true love's accent
If you wouldn't have been the one bringing it to existence
Though I stand confused filled with discontent
That I should feel blessed to know what it means
Or cursed to afford to have you only in my dreams
Cause we are not meant to be
Together in this lifetime and that perhaps kills me
Every time my thoughts wander to the possibilities
Of how 'happiness forever' would actually feel

12

Habits from You

"**A**anya di, since when did you start listening to rock music?" asked my cousin Ronny.

"I didn't realize, our taste keeps changing I suppose," I said lying sheepishly knowing that truth could not be told.

This conversation that I recall now is the one I had during our third year at college when after having been with you for over a year, my playlist accommodated a lot of your taste.

Ronny is my cousin I told you about, the one closest to me and two years younger, he knew a lot about me including the kind of tracks that I loved playing. He is now working in Hyderabad in some IT company after having completed engineering from Chandigarh. My baby brother has grown into a 6 feet tall and handsome man with outstanding features. My aunt is therefore constantly worried about him as she thinks he would fall for any girl's trap soon.

Parents' worries can never have an end. Earlier she used to be apprehensive about whether he would excel in academics and get a decent job and now she is concerned about his partner. Similar concerns most parents have looking at the large number of adults choosing their life partner themselves.

When I met him in the summer break after the third year, he wanted to check any good tracks that he could listen to on my phone and while scrolling he posed that question. We have been very close; he is the only cousin who has been the closest to me. We had played all day even during exams in school time, mocked each other over almost everything and never failed to pull each other's leg, especially before other people.

I certainly miss him as he could have been my strength as he always supported his elder sister. Being a corporate slave now away to Hyderabad he visited only once since I have moved here. He has become quieter. Sometimes on a call, he says,

"Ahh, I don't even realize where the days are going? I am out for work from morning till night. On weekend I get time to cover up my sleep or go out with colleagues. Life is just passing Di; how could I once want this job? Maybe for the good pay check, I traded away life!"

"Who has told you to be a slave to that work there? Come home we will figure out something else for sure." I would always say.

I tell him to come back knowing that isn't a plausible option. He has kept his shoulders to the wheel to first pass the entrance exams and then all through his college years to secure a job in one of the finest IT companies in the country.

What I told him long back then wasn't a complete lie, our taste keeps changing but most of the time it is someone special who brings about that change in our life. Not just about our proclivity but also our values and our perspective about life changes. And so do our propensities some of which we acquire from that someone special.

We acquire habits in countless different ways and one of those many distinct ways is acquiring it from the people around us. I didn't notice it until we parted our ways that there were so many habits, I had acquired from you. So far seem to have adapted your whole lifestyle in a way that even my style of talking is no more my own. It is like we shared each other and acquired a part of each other which we carry within ourselves.

They say that marriage is the union of two people and now I understand how this has been so far justified. A union of mind, soul and body, so acquiring habits is just a little part of what the two of them share. These habits are hard to get out of or maybe it is me who does not want to leave those habits just to keep a part of you alive as an intrinsic part of me.

These habits but make me more miserable as these remind me of you while I have to learn to live without you. Thus again I am left stupefied and just cannot decide. I rebuke myself sometimes when I do a thing your way and sometimes, I would just want to do it only your way.

I am sure that in your absence these habits would also leave with time. But until then I will be stuck in the conundrum of whether to cherish the habits, I've acquired from you or detest them for adding to my miseries.

So all this time I did not realize
How I had acquired habits from you that it did surprise
Your style of talking, expressing love, even your ways of
fabricating lies

Seems like a part of you, I've acquired
Your playlist has now become mine
All the songs we heard together, all the rhymes
Keep playing in my head with the memories in the
background
Leaving me confused, reminding me of the wounds

13

Under the Same Sky?

"Where has grandpa gone papa?"

"Why does he not take us out to buy us chocolates?" the innocent questions of a four-year-old kid to his father.

"Beta, your grandpa has found peace; you can see him in the sky at night"

"The star that shines the brightest is your Grandpa" would be the answer of that kid's father not knowing what else he could tell a four-year-old child. People who have grown up in India can recall at least one such instance where they overheard such conversation after the demise of a loved one.

This was the one that I overheard when I was only seven years old but old enough to understand that our grandfather had passed away and has not become a star. My youngest cousin asked his father a couple of days after my grandfather's demise about his whereabouts crying to meet him.

For some ignorant years, even I was told whenever I asked about any person who was no more between us that the person has turned into a bright star in the sky and is always watching us from above.

Haven't you been told something similar when you were young? I guess that's the way the grownups have always talked about the deceased before any child. That's consoling and not harsh for the child to hear that's why. This is yet another way we deal with harsh truths, we pacify the intensity of damage it can cause if spoken bare

In the later years of life, I understood that it was not just the child who was being consoled by his father but also the father who was trying to console himself by saying it out aloud that his father had at last found peace.

We always have these strange ways of consoling ourselves whenever accepting the truth only leaves us sore. That's when we lie to ourselves because that is more comforting than the truth which stings.

Sometimes despite knowing the truth we live in denial. At times, our ears want to hear the sweet lie when we are aware of the truth.

"How strange is that Romit, despite knowing the truth we prefer to not hear it?"

Then I think what good it would even do to us to be reminded of the bitter truth again. It would only make us sore.

"Ever wondered why do we do that?"

"Does that change the truth in any way?"

No, it does not but accepting it makes things no better so we prefer to deceive ourselves and stay happy. Here I am often reminded of the saying,

'Ignorance is bliss'

Or the popular slogan one says to oneself, 'all is well' even when he is unaware or ignorant of what's happening around.

And that again reminds me of a story that I did not read or hear but witnessed before my eyes. You must have too at some point.

My aunt's mother who showed no signs of any sort of ailment fainted one evening, after having fits she collapsed on the floor. She was rushed to the hospital and no one could even think of what was revealed later. After a couple of days of running different tests and medical procedures, the doctors found she had a cancerous brain tumour and she could hardly survive for three more months.

Nothing was told to her about her ailment, she was ignorant for a few days until the tumour was operated. She was happy for those few days because she was ignorant of what infirmity her body had been nurturing. After the operation of course the mental state deteriorated because it did substantially affect her brain's functioning.

They were all blissful until the truth was revealed and suddenly the happiness was sucked all into an abyss. So ignorance is bliss, right? The time she had here was limited and that could not be altered despite awareness of the illness. So better live blissfully till the last breath rather than brood over the fact that she was going to leave.

If ever someday anything of that sort happens to me then I would just tell myself that all is well and pretend as if everything was normal, I wouldn't let anyone brood over it.

I criticize a lot of things about our society but this rule of consoling, making truth less harsh and more bearable is something I appreciate about society.

One such way which I personally always used when you'd be distant from me, sometimes miles away was that I said to myself

"We both are after all always under the same sky"

"Vague is it Romit?"

"Isn't it vague consolation?"

No, it is perhaps not. I get contented to know that somewhere in this world you exist and are living a good life. The fact of your existence is sufficient to be at peace. Now distance may be the factor that diminishes the amount of peace that I get but still, there is contentment.

It always makes me feel better. Every time I would look up at the sky as if I am in a way looking at you. So even tonight when I was under the night sky, I tried to console myself with the same old trick that never failed.

Though we will always be miles apart this thought that we would after all be under the same sky and you would be safe and sound makes me feel better.

I was strolling up on the roof
With a lot of thoughts, I just wanted some time aloof
The wind was such a relief on the summer night
I continued to walk under the cloudy sky in the quite
With no one around to offer distraction to my rhymes
I could recall the last summertime
Feeling the breeze, I let it flow, all the rhymes
I tried to hear the music of the nature's wind chime
The leaves rustle and the hushed whispers
Seemed to mumble one name in my ears
Separated by miles, the wind acted like a messenger

It carried the message beautifully clear
Were you too strolling under the same sky?
As open sky was as good a treat to you as to my eyes

14

My Favourite Song

"You have to fill this and pass on"

My classmate sitting next to before me said, handing me a sheet of paper which was to be filled with certain details required for board examinations. The registration for appearing in board examinations of tenth grade in our school would begin in eighth grade itself.

"Name, gender, school etc was totally fine but what was 'category' with the following options- GEN, OBC, SC/ST"

I was perplexed; I did not know what it meant. All credits to my poor general knowledge and also my parents who never taught me anything like divisions of human beings based on their caste/category.

"Hey, what are you?" I asked the boy who sat next to me. Sounds uncanny right? Even I think I should have put it in a manner more agreeable to ears. But I was just a kid and I did not know what category was so I did not know how to put that word rightly in a question.

"I am GEN only, I know" he replied with a grin making me doubt if he knew that actually or was just making up.

Anyways I didn't have the option to doubt him, asking another classmate would make me feel more embarrassed than I could bear.

I too marked GEN thinking this is what the majority of my classmates are; maybe I belong to that category only.

Later that day when I reached home, I asked my father,

"Today, they asked us to fill a form in which there was also an option of category"

"What is the category? Which one do we belong to?"

My father replied, "We belong to the general category. The government decides who belongs to which category based on our caste"

I wasn't sure if I registered this thought, I wanted to know what all castes existed, and I always overheard while elders would talk that we are Thakurs (Kshatriya) but which all were the other castes? But I didn't ask anything further.

It was my fear to speak a lot before my father that stopped me. He is a very strict man, true to the definition of an Indian father whose one stern look is as efficient as a rebuke. My father has always been a businessman by profession and my mother a housewife who as a person is the complete opposite of my father, docile, gentle and very soft true to the definition of a mother.

After a few days we were taught in the school itself, the caste division that existed in the past and that which exists in the present which answered the queries that had sprung up a few days ago.

So that is how I first learnt about how we were alienated on this basis. Later with time, I learnt a lot about the dissections that are prevalent in this society. I am grateful to have such parents who never stopped me from playing with those children who belonged to some other caste or religion. They never even introduced me to this idea that there could be any difference between humans on such a social or even economic basis. The only criterion that I was taught was that the human should be good; the only assessment that was to be done was based on his character.

Another thing that I learnt was the divisions were alive not because we wanted them to perpetuate for eternity but because the social structure would not allow us to dissolve them. It is a very complex structure and a change would take years to happen.

Romit, I never told you before or anyone else of this incident then why now?

It's undemanding and effortless for you to appreciate and I know you must have understood. Your parents predominantly resisted our marriage because we did not belong to the same caste. While you were a Brahmin by birth, I was kshatriya. The sourness in our relation too began after your family knew about us which was right before our marriage.

I wish people could understand that it is not the caste or religion of a person that defines him but his actions and his character. I fell in love with you and only you.

Not even a single day passes when I do not think about you, if I were to draw an analogy to describe just how constantly you are on my mind then it would be 'my favourite song', seeing the way it keeps playing in my head consciously or unconsciously at any hour of the day without an option to pause.

The way I get absorbed into the melody of the song is the way I get completely absorbed in reliving you over and over again.

Do we all not have that one favourite song the love for which is not ephemeral and which we never get tired of or weary of, it is very much like we do not get tired of that one person who we love and cherish to hold onto forever. New songs make it up to the lists of the favourite with the trend and also fade away with time only to be replaced with some newer ones but there is something with that one song that is close to our heart that forever remains so.

You are that favourite song for me which can never change. I keep playing our memories and love to lose myself in the ecstasy of playing the happy moments on rewind. It is as if I own the control to play and rewind the memories before my eyes. I however have no pause button on the remote control.

How mind-boggling device it would be if get a remote-control with pause, play and rewind option for life too. Just the way we have it when we play music. I would surely have paused life at the moment we were together.

Sometimes those memories also leave my eyes moist letting my wet eyelashes loudly proclaim the intensity of how much I miss you.

I've long pretended to be alright
It's time to unleash emotions trapped inside
You are stuck in my every surmise
I just can't get things out right
Cause you were my favourite song
I now play every time I am alone

It gets played in my head merely by habit
Whenever I'm left to myself, I'm caught by it
In our days together, I used to rejoice at every beat
It always brought out that passion and heat
It was you who brought my body into motion
Touched and played every emotion

15

<hr>

Look at Yesterday

"Look at how I looked in the first year of college, Aanya"

You would chuckle showing me the same picture, again and again, every few months after college. The picture in which you stood leaning at the life door with that nefarious smile on your face always ready to engage yourself in some mischief. You had that lean body which most guys have when they just enter college, no beard, no moustache, the boyish look on the face.

"Ha-ha, look at the change, I really looked like a clown back then" you would add at times.

And why wouldn't you boast? There was a huge change in your personality. After college, you metamorphosed into a tall, broad and handsome man with a muscular frame of body, those big dark and deep black eyes, broad chest, perfect beard and a full-grown moustache.

The changes were just not external Romit, were they? Your growth was not limited to the external appearance but you grew immensely from within with each passing day and so did I.

One picture from my childhood is clearly etched to my memory, now when I recollect it there is a mixed feeling of vexation, annoyance and also amusement; Amusement because I've grown up too and annoyance because what cannot be accepted should not be accepted.

So I was maybe ten or nine years old and we happened to visit our ancestral village which is somewhere fifty kilometres from Gwalior, my hometown. Not the entire family of my father who all lived in Gwalior but just two of my aunts' family and me and my parents. One of my aunts has a daughter who was then three years old and the other aunt has a son who was then five.

In the village, my father's cousin uncle lived, my grandfather had no siblings so my father had only two cousin uncles. One of them lived in that village and we met him.

Everything was just fine about the visit except when we were departing and heading back to Gwalior, my father's uncle worshipped my cousin brother giving him a hundred rupees note. I'd say worshipped because he applied some vermilion powder on his forehead, sprinkled some rice and performed aarti and also gave him some money.

What did that mean? Was my brother God? I was used to such treatment on the occasion of Navratri when all our neighbours would invite me for lunch which was halwa puri and then they would do the same. Apply some vermilion powder on my forehead, sprinkle some rice, sometimes perform aarti and give us some money. But it wasn't the time of Navratri and moreover, he wasn't a girl.

I asked my mother, "Why is Uncle not doing it for me too?"

"Here in the village, sons and daughters are treated a little differently" she shook her head and clicked her tongue realizing she could have found another excuse but blurted out the truth.

"Don't worry, I will give you something on reaching home" she winked her eye trying to atone for speaking the truth.

As a little child too I could feel and understand the discrimination and I was enraged. All the way back home I did not speak. I even looked at my brother disdainfully because I loved him and still, he would be an accomplice to what just happened. That is how I thought that time as a child when I was embittered.

Why were I and my cousin sister eluded? Because we were girls and he was a boy who would carry the name of this family after my father's generation. This was the logic behind that discriminatory act.

Shouldn't I be ferociously mad at such instances? Yes because it is unacceptable, such a rudimentary thought process. But since I have grown up from the inside too, I find it amusing how people can live their lives in their own created fallacies.

We all grow with each passing day and a year changes a lot people say. Things get so different in a year, we evolve to be a different person altogether, adding up experiences, gathering all that comes along and gradually shedding the memories of the past, letting go the part of ourselves that we start considering redundant. During that interval we make new relations and also let go some old ones, we acquire certain habits and get out of some past ones.

Change is the only constant and so everything too changes for the better. A person who is reluctant to accept life changes only adds up to his troubles. We should embrace change positively; we should grow and evolve.

Whenever I look at the person I was yesterday, I see how I've changed over the years and how it was also paramount to my growth. There are instances from the past reflecting upon which I can't help but laugh after seeing the naivety with which I dealt with situations.

I remember meeting you the first time when we were in college, the first real-time conversation we had is something I would never forget.

Life is so unpredictable, that day I could have never thought that the person who nearly moved me to tears would be the one with who I would choose to spend the rest of my life. Yes, you did, I just never confessed. I did not want you to go through a guilt trip for that.

Some of us sat in the lecture hall after we had our lunch. We still had half an hour before the next lecture would begin.

"Aanya, I have never heard your voice in class, you are so quiet"

Those were the initial days of college when I did not even know all the batch mates.

"Yes, I speak less," I said expressing no interest in talking to you further.

"Do you know how to even yell? Have you ever hurled an abuse?" you continued anyway

"No"

"That's not possible! You must have done that someday."

"I don't"

"Okay then let's try, I will teach you. You just have to repeat after me, alright?"

"Let it go man" Shashank, our batchmate interrupted who was also sitting in the lecture hall and was engaged in a conversation with you until you began with your ridiculous questions to me.

I walked out of the hall. I wondered how people could be so ridiculous in their behaviour. I resolved to not even have the courtesy of a fellow batchmate towards you after that day.

That's how we had our first real conversation. But then my perspective about you changed drastically with time. You just did not know what things were supposed to be said when. You were poor in that aspect and I noticed this all the time.

The picture of that day is so vividly clear, we were so young and I was naïve who had just moved out of the town for the first time, ready to face the real world on my own.

As the days passed so did the experience grows and with that experience did wisdom. You lost your head over for the simple and innocent girl that I was in my last teens and I simply fell for the look in your eyes whenever you would look at me, it was always as if you are looking at magic! It felt that way, as if someone is looking at a magic trick so thoughtfully getting submerged in the thought process.

We never really know what can befall the very next moment; I do not know whether I would complete writing this page, the person reading this may not know if he would read ahead, no one ever knows what may happen next.

The pictures of the past often play before my eyes depicting the transition I've undergone in the past few years. When we look at yesterday, we realize that we have grown with each passing day, embracing everything that comes along.

And whenever I would look at yesterday
I would see how childlike and simple were my ways
That, though I had bettered myself striving each day
Yet been beguiled by the world's deceptive ways
How each one of us feels the same way?
We all grow and learn from yesterday
Adding memories which we preserve in the closet
Or those that come to life from the pictures tucked in the
pocket
Just a glimpse and we relive the moment
Feel the gush of every emotion that needed to be spoken
As if some magic wand performing a reversion
Showing us our young and dumb version

16

Merely hearts

A homeless and destitute child hugs a rich kid and the rich toddler embraces him back with a warm and comfortable smile like kin embracing each other and the video goes viral and circulates all over the social media.

"What was so exceptional about the video Romit that it caught so much attention?"

It seemed so ordinary, just two little kids hugging each other, displaying human affection most warmly. Isn't that what the norm is supposed to be? If we both were to settle on this, I know we would call this the standard norm which is expected in society. We sure have different tastes when it comes to all things external but on the inside, we share the same values.

But is that the reality? No.

Humans are viewed from the lens of social status, economic status and political status by other humans. It is some sort of filter lens that filters out the humans on the materialistic yardstick. We all wear this lens; it develops gradually over years. We are not born with this filter lens because the creation does not demand it; the body only needs the lens we are born with.

When all the parameters are at par then two people can develop and show affection for each other but not otherwise.

The two kids in the video were not at par when seen from the focal point of their societal position. So what made this video go viral was the fact that one child was seen as a poor and homeless kid at the lowest end of the social strata while the other kid at its highest end and defied the rules of segregation of the society.

They were only humans with no labels at that moment. So each affair has been made complex because of the complex differences. Society has complex problems today and all those are man-made. Man has himself invented these problems.

As far as affection is concerned, public display of affection is a crime per se as per some radical elements of the society whereas commission of the crime itself in public is pardonable. Though we are apart, I know you must be aware of the pitiable situation in our country.

In our society, even marriage is not the union of two humans who love each other and yearn to spend the rest of their lives with each other. Marriage in this society is predominantly a complex affair and perhaps under the hold of many social evils. Inter-caste marriages and inter-religious marriages are still taboo for the majority of the section of the society and are prevented by societal pressure, parental pressure, religious conservatism and casteism.

If I would talk of the other social evils which annihilate the sanctity and piousness of this union, I would have to numb myself prior to expounding on the matter as being a woman I know how much more do these evils plague our lives. How women are left at the mercy of their in-laws, their families made to pay dowry and their bodies burnt alive. The misery seems to end only at the end of a woman's life.

You and I both are already aware of the social evils that hound the institution of marriage. Speaking explicitly of the inter-caste marriage is a little important because who can know about it better than us as we have been the victim of this rudimentary practise that has been followed for years?

The lack of support for our decision was because we belonged to a different caste and that was ridiculous in my opinion. We were adamant though and nevertheless did not give up our choice. We were fortunate to belong to well to do families who though did not wholeheartedly consent to our marriage also did not resort to some drastic measures to part us away.

Today, while reading the articles I came across one such incident which narrated the plight of two lovers who belonged to different castes and were brutally murdered by the families in the name of the honour of the family name. I will never understand the inhumanity inflicted in the name of the artificial social barriers created between men. How can one forget to be a human above belonging to a community, caste or religion?

Under such prevailing circumstances in the country, I feel blessed to be brought up in a family which accepted my marriage though a little less wholeheartedly but eventually their happiness lied in mine.

The incident in the news also made me recall the few early days of emotional trauma and distress that we had to go through in the beginning, whenever I hear of such similar stories, I feel the pain that they must have to go through because

> *Those are merely hearts*
> *Which would beat for the other one even when apart*
> *They do not know the labels of any caste*
> *Which could become the reason to draw them apart*
> *Are the labels so fundamental to existence?*
> *That these could put an end to love in an instant?*
> *So what then follows is always a tragedy*
> *Written with words which could describe the catastrophe*

17

Ode to My Lover

"Aanya, you know compromise is crucial for a relationship to nourish," my mom told me.

It was a fine evening; I felt good and was strolling on the terrace. She joined me a few minutes later intending to talk.

"I understand Ma"

"This generation does not understand that. Our distant relatives you know the ones who own the central mall in this city have three daughters. All of them are nearly thirty now. They married the eldest daughter last year and she got separated from her husband after a few months of marriage. The young generation does not want to adjust at all"

"Ma, do you mean a woman has to adjust?" I said a little irritated

"No, Aanya. I mean both of them to need to, just because you are a woman does not mean that only you would but you would have to as well."

"I get it. It is not just about marriage but every relation."

"We want you to marry someone again and we would not want that you give up easily on your future relation"

"Hmmmm" I said not willing to spark up the argument on a second marriage.

The brevity of particularly every one of the relations today cannot be overlooked as most of the relations seem to be falling apart.

Most of the people have lost what is needed to keep a relation last for long if not forever. Acceptance, understanding, unselfishness and keeping the ego aside are some of the fundamentals needed for any healthy relationship.

"Why don't you speak, Romit?"

"I've told you; you need to eat Aanya"

And then there was only silence for thirty minutes all that time while we sat together at the same table in their college mess. The air was not quite though; the commotion of the people around us in the mess was at its pinnacle, it being dinner time. In any case, we didn't talk by any means.

You would not speak because I refused to have dinner that night. And I could not find words to convince you that I was not hungry at all.

There was pure anger and concern on your face that day. It was the first time that I saw these two emotions together being reflected plainly from your face as if no effort was made to hide any. There were so many instances later when I saw that demeanour all over again on your face but that evening was the first time. As you know Romit how exceptional 'the firsts' are that those moments are etched clearly in our memory.

After having noticed that, my eyes turned a little moist as I was so moved by your concern. It had only been a few days since we started talking and our feelings welled up, making an obvious show on your face. I was also a little scared to speak anything considering how irate you looked and sounded.

I feel that it is my greatest loss to not have you anymore besides me, someone for whom my well being and happiness topped the list of priorities, and someone whose eyes would not look for anyone else and whose heart would always yearn for my company.

I have lost significant weight and my cheeks look a little sunken which implies that the effect is perceptible on the face too. I have also noticed that I have to use the bathroom more often. Don't know what is wrong with this body.

Maybe it is only the deprivation of your love. If you were here today, I know you would have been mindful of what is happening. Your concern for me far outweighed mine. You were as strict as my father when the question was about my health. You would never take a 'no' as an answer to anything about my well being. And if I would refuse for anything then that face of yours would resurface.

When we were together there were a few things for which I should have apologized at the ideal time and maybe that could have saved our relationship.

We frail humans often take up the contention that it was the other's slipup too so why should we only apologize or why should we make an apology first. That is where we take the erroneous and misguided direction that often leads us to ruin our relations.

What we should always follow is that the relationship is between two people no matter whosoever is at fault, if the relation gets jeopardized then it is the loss of both and not just one. Both would suffer by the same token and then the question of who should have asked for forgiveness first or at all would only haunt them in the future. There will be no turning of the clock back and all that will be left will be regret.

The way I sometimes keep asking for your apologies in your absence in the absurd hope of getting things right relentlessly day and night,

How I could get things right
For days I tried hard to write
As I really wanted to apologize
Because I was not by his side
Whenever he needed me the most
At times when he was lost
All alone left to himself to battle
Against the people, against his own problems all which he
had to tackle
I wasn't aware of the damages I had caused
And he didn't complain at all, never mentioned my flaws
His love was still standing strong
Like a firm sapling against windstorm
This sapling had faced only adversities since its dawn
But he acted like a shield protecting it all by himself even
when I was gone
Though together we had planted it but I couldn't hang on
I wasn't as strong as him to face the thunderstorms
If I be allowed, I just want to be his ointment
Over all the bruises he has suffered as atonement
No words can suffice my feelings right now or ever
Still I try it in this ode to my lover

18

Beautiful Today

"You look so beautiful today Aanya" the first compliment I received from you.

"What was special today that you noticed?" I pondered and inquired

"The way that you wore this suit" you replied

"I will get more of those in my wardrobe," I said grinning; glad to know what you preferred.

That was the day when for the very first time I wore a suit to college and that is how I came to know that you liked me more in those. Usually, I would put on any casual western outfit but that day you would not take your eyes off me. You did not compliment me the other days, it was the first time I grabbed all your attention.

I form a conjecture at times that it is every woman who wants to look beautiful for her man. But, that must be a fraction only of the women around the globe. Whenever I would put on your favourite colour or the traditional dresses that you loved to see me in, I would wait anxiously for you to notice and compliment me. I would consistently desire to look beautiful for you; it was as if all the adornments that I would apply were only because I would want to catch your eye.

This inclination was even more grounded at the outset of our relationship when we would have only a few hours with each other and those were the college hours. Yes, the time of our lives when we had just met and started seeing each other often. Do I need to remind you that it was seven years back from now when we were fresher in the college? I would always want to look my best or just the way you wanted to see me. I would love to put on your favourite dresses and stringently no cosmetics because you despised it above all.

It was a magical feeling being around you and I guess it was the other way round for you too as you would likewise put on the colours that I loved. This desire to look good and beautiful when around you was explicable or rather inexplicable, I really don't know. I never happened to talk about this feeling with any other woman but I also never failed to notice just how they would want to look their best whenever they went out with their love. I assume it is not just me who wanted to look beautiful for her man.

I always questioned my mother why she would never add any make-up to her skin and it was the monotonous reply that I was served every time, guess what?

"Your father doesn't really like makeup at all"

And thus mother would never apply any. So this is the story of almost every married couple or lover, each would want to look beautiful the way one's counterpart would like to see them.

My mother's sister, my aunt on the other hand would not step out of the house without embellishments she could apply to add to her beauty. She would doll up in western attire only contrary to my mother who would never try any adornments and no attire which was not Indian. Sisters nurtured and fostered in the same house by the same parents in the same family yet had different inclinations towards dressing up for the bare reason that they would do it as it pleased their husbands.

All these years with you I would also dress the way you adored and almost forgot how I would have relished to see myself.

You know how out of my proclivity I would still dress the way you liked me to and how each time it would just remind me that you are no longer here to see me and compliment me. This would add up to my misery again and I would just not want to even look at my reflection in the mirror. To be honest, since you left, the desire to look any good or beautiful too faded away.

I contemplated and realized just how wrong it is for a woman to want to be her best only for her man. It should be for her that she should take care of her body, health and beauty. In Indian philosophy or traditions, this particular thought has been propagated for ages that a woman should do all she can to make her husband happy and this idea percolates down to keeping up the appearance as per the choice of her husband.

I feel this behaviour of ours to always look good in the way our partner wants us to is genetic. The inclination has just been inherited. I feel that very wrong, a woman who should have bodily autonomy should be free to choose the way she wants to keep her external appearance rather than being told how she must keep it.

I am not talking of those who happily and wilfully wish to confirm to the choice of their partners as was my case but those who are taught that they have to do it and do so under societal pressure.

Romit, you have always sought my happiness and I'm so glad to tell you that today after many years I felt beautiful without associating the feeling with someone else's compliments or notice as I accidentally happened to catch an eye of my reflection.

I am sure you would have been happy to know that I,

Just felt beautiful today
As I caught the sight of my reflection in that shallow pond
that was on the way
The soothing wind made my hair sway
The orange hue of the sky in those evening hours of the
day
Made it all so picturesque, like a beautiful portrait
I sat, kneeling next to the pond
Allowing myself to relish the lost beauty that I had found
Which was all along just within
Though I for long failed to see anything
Today nature played the role of cupid
And made me feel the love for myself, to which I had been
secluded

19

Anyone Else But You

"It is time; they must be arriving soon why you aren't ready Aanya?" told my mother surprised to see me still in bed.

Looking at the table clock which was not working she exclaimed, "It is not working; we got batteries at home, why didn't you change?"

I was quiet, did not speak and this is how I had been all these days. And what could I even say? The time for me stopped since we parted our ways, days and nights only passed as they were obliged to follow the ritual of nature. For me life was on hold, I only existed at that moment, but was not alive.

The clock only symbolized how time was stuck for me and did not move. In a way, I felt it displayed reinforcement to my feelings. Why would I then attempt to discredit my clock by changing its batteries? An inanimate object comprehended and showed solidarity when the living breathing humans bestowed with emotions could not.

It didn't even matter what time of the day it was as I did not work or go out on any occasion so keeping track of time was of no good use to me. While I was ruminating my mother waited for a reply.

Finally, her patience broke and she said, "You have ten minutes, get ready before they arrive"

'Though my loss of interest in almost everything is explicable but I have difficulty eating food. Like I mentioned earlier the loss of appetite, I am fatigued all the time and that makes me look sick'

I anyhow got myself out of bed and did my hair and nearly no makeup except for the lip shades in the absence of which I looked sick. It is not that looking sick troubled me but who would listen to my parent's rant later on. I could do the bare minimum for my parents.

I need not narrate what followed later as that is wholly irrelevant; the guests who were expected at our house were Sumit's uncle and aunt who lived in our city. Sumit is the guy my parents want me to marry. He works as a software engineer in Bangalore, I would not comment on his physical appearance as I once barely saw his photograph on the consistent insistence of my parents. As you know this would be my second marriage and the groom was chosen accordingly, someone who had been looking for a partner for a considerable amount of time that he has no issues marrying a divorcee. I had already denied this proposal of my parents but since this meet was already decided so it was all just a formality before we could expressly say no.

Romit, have you ever noticed that you are sometimes clung to something that you love in a way that even if better things are offered in exchange you would pick the one you have developed a fondness for.

It's like being that adamant child who cries for his favourite toy that has been broken, he wants that particular toy back again at any costs above anything else that is offered to him. This applies likewise in the case of a person too; you want only that person for whom you have developed affinity, no matter if someone better wishes to walk in your life.

The prospect of marrying again had left me numb. My parents proposed the idea of getting remarried as I had my entire life ahead of me. It is but obvious, isn't it? When you have just entered your late twenties and are separated from your husband after a couple of years of marriage then your family would want you to marry again and so did mine too. But how was I supposed to deal with the past that hadn't yet left me, that which I relived again and again in my mental frame?

For me, time never actually moved ahead. It was stuck in that last moment that we had together.

Like a little adamant child even I want you back in my life over anything else. Sincerely if you ask me, I haven't moved on at all and to think of someone else is nothing short of infidelity for me. My family wants me to decide soon as I would be acceptable before I reach the age of thirty. They do not even wish to allow me some time to grieve over the relationship that has just ended and begin a new one.

I am still clung to you and wish to remain so with no desire now or in the future to move on with someone else,

> *Days and months have passed by*
> *I still remember our entire story, don't understand why*
> *Time seems to have lost its power*
> *I think of you in every possible hour*

The memories of us as fresh as a newly blossomed flower
Not fainted or blurred in any part
What is it that works even when we are miles apart?
Change of time, place, people nothing seems to work on
this heart
Which is adamantly clung to you
And denies accepting anyone else but you

20

Maybe Someday

"If Romit likes traditional dresses so must his family" I told myself while deciding on what to wear for lunch at your place. Your family lived in Delhi itself and I had long waited to meet your parents. I had heard stories from you and the curiosity had reached its peak.

Then I did put on a blue kurta, that kurta being one of my favourites and the colour is one of your favourites. I wanted to look fine.

The first time during our courtship years when you called me home, it was during our fourth year of college. I was nervous because of the many stories I had heard about your father. He seemed to be stricter than mine and then I felt it maybe natural, he being a retired army officer.

We met at your place on the pretext of preparing for the exam that was two days later. You went home as we had plenty of holidays for exam preparation. After having lived in the city for a year you felt commuting everyday from home to college was exhausting and thus you lived in the campus for the next four years.

We studied for a while and then your mother called us to have lunch. Well, you were not going to introduce me as your prospective future wife at that point intime. I was introduced as your fellow batchmate and friend.

Your mother is a lovely kind woman, just like any other mother on this planet. Why are all the mothers so lovely? Sometimes I feel maybe it is right that mothers are the ones God has sent in his absence on Earth to shower fathomless love and at the same time are fiercely protective for their children.

"Have another chapatti; you eat so less, that is why you are so thin" she would say after every couple of minutes while I ate.

"Romit also does not eat well these days; don't know what is wrong with you children?" she talked while I would just sit quietly nodding and smiling at her remarks.

"No sweets? You don't like?" she asked looking amazed by the fact that I took none out of the four different kinds that she served.

"No auntie, I don't eat sweets a lot," I said in a low voice already full.

There is another peculiar thing about Indian mothers that no matter how much her child eats she would always find it less, she would always see him as a lean malnourished child who is in dire need of food, food that she would cook herself. I noticed that in almost all the mothers I had met till date.

The very first conversation with your mother made me feel that it would be great to have two mothers in a lifetime. I felt at ease. Your father too smiled in a lovable manner very much contradictory to his nature that one could infer from the stories you narrated. Though he didn't talk but his smile was warm and welcoming when I greeted him that day.

Romit, it is strange we generally remember the very first moments or the last ones or very special ones with people. These days I recall 'the first' moments of everything because I still hope the last ones are yet to happen.

I would get up each day with the hope that it would get better as the days would pass; after all it is only hope that keeps you going in the trying times. As the hours would pass, the hope that I had in the morning would also dwindle and by the time the day was gone, I would feel hopeless, this vicious cycle of getting new hope at the beginning of the day and losing it at the end of it would just go on.

I am but resolute that someday things would not be as harsh as they are today. I have learned just how important hope is in one's life. It gives us sustenance in the darkest of times, just like a ray of light no matter how faint that light maybe yet it gives us the strength to endure the darkness. It saves us from giving in to despair and depression. So even if my hope becomes faint at the end of the day, I choose to believe that there will be another day that would bring blessings and do away with my pain.

At times I don't feel justified to feel the way I do when I see what people go through in their lives. Some people struggle to make both ends meet, people who are born with disabilities, people who live in destitution, misery and who live a life not worth being called human life.

I, on the other hand, feel depressed by the mere fact of being parted with the love of my life. The many struggles of the people out there compel me to forget my pain and even forbid me to lament. But just as everyone has his own story and struggles so do I and mine are centred on the emotional trauma caused by your absence.

It is so wrong I feel, being self-absorbed by your narrow interests and misery. I detest this trait of mine but then isn't that human nature? I try to fight this nature and think beyond this self-centred trauma.

I am learning to cope up with it and hope is something I don't want to give up as I would submit to despair without it. Even in the face of adversity, one can cling to hope as it is only hope that would make one pull through the adversities.

They call hope as a ray of light at the end of a dark tunnel as it that light that makes one continue walking through the dark tunnel. So when everything seems to have been lost it is hoped that helps us survive.

And thus I say,

Maybe someday,
I wouldn't feel like I do today
Terribly alone,
With no desire to continue this on my own
Everything would make sense
I would not continue under the pretence
These days and nights
Would once again excite
I would do away with the emptiness inside
That devours and feeds upon my spirits at times

21

A Thousand Rhymes

"Yes I heard the news, he ran away" my father was almost whispering in an attempt to let his voice not reach anyone's ears.

"Umm, I don't know Mr Parmar" he said with a perplexed look on his face shrugging his shoulders. And then bid adieu to his friend Mr Parmar.

We sat at the dining table in the dining room which is equidistant from my room and my parents' room. We were having dinner as usual when papa's phone rang up. Mr Parmar lives behind our house, in the same neighbourhood and has been a good friend of my father ever since we moved in this place.

Who ran away? I thought to myself but then it was better to not ask anything. Who would want to then listen to the moral lecturing?

My mother filled me in with the details of the incident later that night. It was our distant neighbour Raju. Everyone would always speak behind his back that he was gay observing his mannerism but he did not expressly mention anything about his sexual orientation. Raju as far as I know him is a decent man, he is two years elder to me and I have seen him grow up since he was eleven as that is when his family moved into our neighbourhood.

I was a naïve child back then and did not know much about the LGBTQ community, my age being only nine. I once asked, "Papa, Raju walks like a girl, isn't it funny?"

My father did not find it amusing and said, "Everyone has his style of walking, we should not comment"

That is when I learnt a partial lesson of non-judgment. We are no one to judge anyone for anything. I love my friends and I cherry-picked them for the same reason and also you Romit, you guys don't judge anyone for anything.

He ran away after a week of being seen with one of his male friends in a compromising situation. It was someone from the neighbourhood only who saw them on Raju's terrace and told his father. Raju had to answer many questions and face the wrath of his father. The word did spread like a wildfire; the disseminator of this news was the one who had informed Raju's father.

It is a town with people who still have not modernized in their thought process and stick to the narrow-minded approach of non-acceptance to anything non-confirming to the traditional norms made it hard for him to even walk out of the house with a head held high. Everyone would mock him and make him feel miserable.

"Which times are we living in? Isn't that your question now Romit?"

I would say time depends a lot on the place you inhabit. You can go a hundred years back or even more if born in a tribal community that lives in a forest even today in India though it is not very common considering the diminishing area under forests. You can live in the present age of technology and modernization if you are born in a megacity of the world. So which time we are living in is determined also by which place we live in and not just the number of revolutions earth completes around the sun.

"But is running away a good option? Not talking in reference of my neighbour but generally running away from your problems does any good?"

Every society has its problems; we just fail to acknowledge those until we become a part of that society. We can only observe what is wrong in our immediate surroundings and not what is wrong outside the periphery of those surroundings.

Romit, our society judges a person by the money he has earned, the social or political status that he holds and how big of a name he has earned over the years of his life. If Raju too was an influential and rich figure no one would have bothered him on his personal life.

We are moving towards a materialistic society. It is one of the fundamental and newest developed flaws which pushes people to strive to meet these criteria of success so shallow. They forget the essence of being human, they forget that they are supposed to live life, enjoy every moment while they are chasing the materialistic goals and running a never-ending race.

There are few who understand the depth of what life means, there are few black sheep of the families who chase their passion which makes them feel alive and enjoy every moment they spend while living for what they love. The

Indian society however offers resistance towards accepting such people who do not conform to the normal standards set. They struggle each day to defend their choice.

"Have you ever imagined what happens when this purpose is taken away?"

How does it feel to wake up one day and realize that all the dreams that you've lived for all this while will never turn into reality? One who has suffered the loss of their heart's utmost desires would surely understand. One gets ravaged by one's unfulfilled dreams.

It can be the most devastating thing that can happen to a person as it tends to take away the purpose which keeps one going.

We all want to have a purpose in life, we tend to live a life that has a meaning and for that we set goals and dream about things we want to accomplish. When these dreams are not fulfilled life seems to become meaningless. A perpetual state of disappointment results with each passing day and that results in utter despair and depression. One simply falls in the depths of despair or numb oneself to feel just anything.

I too feel like I am sinking and reaching the depths of despair without you. It is not unusual to find one to be greatly attached to a person and find meaning around them. I've seen a lot of people who are reduced to being 'living dead bodies' after the demise of their loved ones. Out of the two choices at my disposal is either being numb and feeling nothing at all or the other one to submit to the depression that this state of despair would lead me to, I have not yet made a choice.

I still hope that we may still anyhow live together and be happy like we had always wanted. I have clung to the hope and not accepted the truth. Whenever I write, I hope that someday you would read all my rhymes and come back saying that you have missed me every moment of every day since we had parted just like the way I did.

There is no other way left to me to express just how much I need you and how badly I want you again. I bleed with words in the hope that these would bring you back, clinging to the vague hope as you would not even get to read the memoir still,

I try to write a thousand rhymes
That might bring you back in my life
But I doubt if you too want the same
Or you would just say it was all me to blame
Can I create another beautiful piece without reprise?
That would surely leave you surprised
Anything, whatever it takes to get to you
Your absence has left me black and blue
I wouldn't care about a thing this time
As long as you would say that you're mine
I traded off happiness back that time
It was you always who made me smile
Can I get that back or is it too late?
Would you answer my call, if I call you mate?

22

The Road

'Every flower that blooms has to fade away, that's the thing about everything beautiful, it is destined to doom after a while.'

Therefore, grieving over that which is unavoidable is adding self-inflicted misery to the already piled up stock of afflictions that the world offers. One should be sagacious enough to make peace with the transient nature of everything in the world. Nothing lasts forever, for that which is born death is certain and everything that finds its creation is bound to find destruction.

"Is that all?" the doctor asked

"Yes," I replied with my heart racing already.

My father impelled me to visit a gynaecologist after having observed my weight loss and the unbearable pain I would have during my menstrual cycles. He booked an appointment and told my mother to accompany me. I however insisted on going alone. I wrote to you earlier about the loss of appetite and the sunken cheeks. Now the list has gotten long. I did not wish to worry my parents more; there were already enough reasons for emotional tension.

I accordingly went to a gynaecologist on the scheduled time and date.

"What symptoms you have been experiencing lately?" the doctor asked

"Be very careful not to miss any, tell me about everything that you experience" she added after a brief pause.

"Loss of appetite, bloating, indigestion, abdominal fullness, I mean I feel full too soon, I am not able to eat much. Pain in the lower abdominal area," I said taking my time to recall all the symptoms.

"And also weight loss" I added

After having thought for a minute more while she was contemplating, I finally added one more,

"Also I think I need to use the bathroom frequently. So frequent urge to urinate?"

"Is that all?" she asked again

"Yes," I firmly said.

"We shall run through some basic tests first, if there would be anything peculiar that we should be worried about then we might have to run some special tests further." She said trying not to make me anxious.

The reason my father strictly sent me was that these symptoms were experienced by a woman who are diagnosed with ovarian cancer. He read it in some newspaper article and that is what perturbed him. I was certain there was no such problem with my health and it was just the emotional turbulence in my life that took a toll on my health.

How could I be diagnosed with such a thing, that's nearly impossible? I still firmly believed all of this to be normal, anyone can experience this and the majority of the people have these minor complaints.

Romit, I have just lost the appetite for life in your absence. That is what I feel is also the justification for the show of bodily symptoms. But for the sake of my father's satisfaction, I consulted the doctor.

Romit our journey is beautiful to me in many ways, the most beautiful time of my life. I cannot express the gratitude that I hold for being blessed with some moments of ecstasy, unbound happiness in your presence. This is how I sum up the time that we had spent together but we are both aware of the many peaks and valleys that were a part of the journey we had set together.

I always would question that why being with someone could be so difficult? Why each time hurdles would lie all along the way? The memories are just so vivid that I can recall all the events of our life that I felt each time that a jinx had been cast upon us.

I can bet that if written down, ours would also make a great love story like Romeo Juliet or Laila Majnu with the only exception that neither of our lives has ended, at least not yet.

If I would begin writing our story then that would take a lifetime for me. I would not take the pain because you and I both know all the things that happened so far, all that you do not know is how I feel right now and that's precisely what I want you to know, for which I write every night. When I look back upon the rough road that we walked, this is how I wish to put it away,

The road we walked was never smooth anyway
It was rugged filled with potholes all along the way
With a scorching sun to add some more to our plate
We never could complete the journey, we were late
There were reasons, there were people and what not to blame
It was a struggle for us to stand together against their game
The potholes were so ingeniously designed
It felt like universe conspired to see us divide
And we got astray adding to the mistakes already in a pile
Like everything beautiful destined to doom after a while

23

You, on My Mind

I told my gynaecologist to personally call me and not my father in any case as they had my father's number too because I wanted to deal with this thing on my own. And I received a call from her this morning.

"Aanya, we would have to run a TUVS (Transvaginal Ultrasound) and CA-125 blood test"

"Mind you come to the hospital today itself?" she didn't sound as calm as she did two days back when I visited her.

"Yes, sure," I said with a pounding heartbeat.

I was not aware of what these tests were; I heard the names for the first time although ultrasound seemed familiar, my internal organs were going to be inspected that was for sure. So this was something not frivolous, I just hoped it was not what we doubted.

The first thought on my mind after the call was yours Romit. I wanted to see you and cry in your arms because I was truly scared. I was scared by the fact that you were still not around and all this was happening. Life could get very cruel at times. My thoughts gave rise to fear at that moment.

We keep thinking about something or the other all the time whether we are consciously aware of those thoughts or not. Most of us are not even aware of our thoughts most of the time. The important part is that our thoughts control the way we feel at that moment, it can make us feel sad, happy, frustrated, lonely, confident, angry, excited, depressed and whatnot. Our feelings are associated with the thoughts that run in our heads. Every feeling is the direct outcome of our thoughts.

Many times people around me ask what I am thinking about to which my reply is always 'nothing' and that is because I am not even consciously aware of what goes on in my head. There's a lot on our minds and we all come across this situation when we say 'nothing' on being questioned as to what is on our mind. All this realization dawned upon me in the past few months of despair.

My thoughts being restricted to you and the grief of not having you in my life anymore, the feeling of despair and depression is a natural consequent to the same. One of the many efforts to not fall into a depressed state of being was to monitor my thoughts as well. So I began with all the thought controlling techniques sold by renowned psychologists across the world but that was no good at all. It is easier said than done and speaking of the thought controlling methods is far too easy to be said than done. We are frail human beings who get swayed easily.

Next, I took up the advice of the near and dear ones more experienced than me and when they said to keep yourself occupied and surrounded by people to avoid thoughts that you want to avoid, I did the same. An empty mind is a devil's tool, I agree to it more than anything.

After analyzing just how much I keep thinking about you all the time I'm left alone to myself, I agree with the above proposition. As a result of trying the methods the world suggested of keeping busy and stuff, I expected the thoughts to be kept in check. On the contrary, there wasn't a change for the better, along with everything else that was on my mind, you still topped the place.

There seems to be no remedy left to cure me of the sickness that leads me to think about you just all the time. Despite trying anything and everything, my thoughts are centred on you, even if I add a lot of things to think about, still, the one constant thought that still hovers is you.

Innumerable things have occupied my mind
But you are at the top, is that fine?
I've tried over a hundred ways
But you still remain in my head anyway
Since morning till I doze off at night
One constant thought pesters me all time
The blurred pictures of us give me chills
Leaving me numb, in need of some pills
You were some drug I got addicted to, badly
I was so down for you, sadly
Were you down for me just like I was for you?
I want to ask once, though I know the answer too

24

Upheaval

"Does everything hold true universally for all the people, Romit?"

No, things work differently for different people. Nothing works in the same manner for two different persons. The degree of variation might be minute or even negligible but the effect is always different.

That day I visited the hospital for the prescribed tests. I had no thoughts; I was blank when I was walking in and while the doctor's staff performed the tests I was told about on the call.

After a few days, the reports had also arrived. Before leaving that day, I had once again instructed the doctor to keep things between me and her only and not let my family know anything about it.

Then I visited the hospital to meet the doctor after the reports had arrived.

"Please, sit," she said with some nervousness on her face.

"I should expect bad news?" I asked plainly with no emotions on my face.

"Well, you know some more tests are required before we reach to any conclusion and biopsy is crucial to determine the nature of the problem"

Biopsy? I thought to myself, isn't that required to ascertain whether the patient has cancer? Did I hear it right? Were my father's doubt right? A flood of thoughts arose in my head.

"Hmm, I shall do that but not in this city, thank you doctor" and I left.

I said that having controlled the flood of thoughts and found a plausible way out. It was as if I entered the building with an empty head knowing well what was waiting inside. On my way back home, I decided that I would shift somewhere else as soon as possible before my parents get to know more about my deteriorating condition. We have always lived in the Gwalior district of Madhya Pradesh, a state in India. Now I decided I would move to some other state to avoid frequent visits from any of my family members.

I reached home.

"What did the doctor say? Did she prescribe any medication?" asked my mother who was actually biding her time for me only.

"Yes, some imbalance in the hormones and nothing else, she has given some tablets" I lied.

"Also, it has been eight months since I left my job and came home, I have decided I would move to Ahmedabad where I have been offered a job with decent pay and accommodation is also provided by the company."

"Well, that's good, but could you not find a job anywhere near or in the same state itself?" my mother said with clear concern on her face.

"No, for now, let me move, I shall keep searching for one in Madhya Pradesh"

That was it, the time I had spent at home was coming to an end and I had no idea what lay ahead, what my reports would say.

So I finally moved out of my town, to another state and started a new job. It is a new city in a different state and a whole new group of people around me sounds quintessential for leaving the past behind however I did not know how long this was going to last. I had been thinking of it since the beginning, since I shifted to my parents' house I started applying for jobs in faraway states, far from every place to which we had been even if it was for once. I just did not wish to have anything around to hold me back from moving on.

This is how anyone ideally tries to get along with life especially if the desire is to get over everything that was in the past. I did the same. But in my case now I did not know how much of life was left. Now the objective of moving here had changed, it was more to conceal anything more about me that would be excruciating for my parents.

It has now been three days since I shifted to this alien land among strange people and guess what? Nothing seems to have changed at all. Despite having nothing around to remind me of the past, my thoughts are still clung to you and everything that is about you and even more so after having discovered a foreboding.

What does it really take to get along with life?

Should I look for answers online?

Or should I consult a psychologist to figure out how I should deal with my mental dilemma of mine?

I have no answers and neither do I have anyone who would help me get the answers to them. It seems like the whole idea of shifting to a new place has only added to the loneliness and despair. There are no familiar faces with whom I share any heartfelt connections and that makes me feel all alone, no better than how I was at home, there I could not express how I felt and here there is no one I can express myself to.

All my efforts thus seem to be in vain, there hasn't been a change. And I haven't visited any hospital since I have come. I am too scared to do that.

One thing that is good about the place is that I can cry myself aloud and there is no one to bother, it just lets me unleash the grief held inside. It is alike an upheaval that I deal with every night, after coming from work when there is the silence of the last hours of the night, it devours my spirits. Can you imagine how it would be like to be all alone in the dead hours of the night when the world sleeps soundly and I am left to be haunted by your memories?

I can't really take it anymore,
Every moment it becomes so hard to endure
Changed places and even people around
So that your memories won't ever hound
Until today when I ran into your words
And memories played one after another with every verse
It just does not make sense anyhow
Why I had kept distance then and even now
As all my efforts have proved to be in vain
It's all a mess, alike the one left after a heavy rain
The heart sank as it does on hearing the thunder roar
The eyes flooded with tears like the waves on the shore

I went back to feeling the upheaval inside
Of the emotions, which had run dried?
I couldn't even think if it was you or your memories
Those made me feel that life without you was full of
miseries
Maybe I just don't know what I want
But I know I've been acting as if nonchalant
Untouched, unmoved and left with no desires
Leaving behind all love, carving a line of fire

25

The Last Ray

Do you know the present-day thing that has been added to my list that I dread the most now? I don't think you would be able to make a guess, as you never could understand me, Romit. Despite knowing that you did not understand me, I signed up for your companionship for life and I guess that's where it went wrong. Anyway, I am not analyzing what went wrong or where we are both flawed.

Anxiousness takes over me as the sun starts setting on the horizon, with every disappearing ray the anxiety starts rising and with complete darkness, I am taken over by complete restlessness. Anxiety, I never thought that I would know what it feels like to be a victim of, on experiencing it myself.

'I feel like the end is near. The sunset symbolizes end and on seeing the sunset in the horizon I feel the end is inevitable and so near'

I keep myself occupied all day with worldly affairs and worries; it's not after all a cakewalk for a single woman to survive in this cruel world. Women face a lot of discrimination in our society in different forms. At home, at the workplace and anywhere where they would dare express their opinion and right and claim that they are humans too and deserve to be treated at par with men.

Now I have to be even more careful about my safety because I virtually know no one here or in the entire state to reach out to me in case I need. As I have been allotted accommodation in the company's building only, there is less to worry about. It is a secure society; my building's watchman is dutiful and also seems like a good man.

Although Ahmedabad is relatively safer when compared to other cities of India still it does not rule out all possibilities of any mishappening to a woman. The heinousness of the crimes that these days are committed against women sends a chill down my spine. I feel fearful of stepping out of the apartment sometimes or trusting anyone.

My mind does not hover over anything else all day with the people around me and with my responsibilities towards myself and the job. It however changes at night; I get the space and time which I do not want and then I willingly or unwillingly reflect upon my past and the impending danger lurking inside my body. Now that I have been avoiding something inevitable, I feel like I am not doing justice to myself.

"Will not getting diagnosed stop the ailment that my body is harbouring and which is possibly even growing every day?"

"Romit, if you would have been here today, maybe I would have wanted to recover and survive too"

These silent hours of the night speak the loudest to me and remind me of you and the moments we spent together. The silence is so strong that it consumes me. I am paralyzed at times and still motionless with my gaze fixed at any corner of the room, I sit folding my arms around my legs, trying to form a layer as if protecting myself from something. The other times I would get my eyes flooded with tears for hours before I finally fall asleep. The eyes in the morning would speak of the torture that was inflicted upon them last night.

I dread the night and its silence and darkness more than any child. It scares me on the whole. The next day is the same and passes in the everyday chores which steal away the time letting me survive and then comes the fall of the day which I dread but pass anyway.

But I would visit a hospital soon; my body seems to be frail now. The condition is deteriorating and soon people would be able to tell that I am sick.

Every last ray of the sun
Which the eye catches in the horizon
Marking the fall of the day
And inviting darkness with the disappearance of
the last ray
Would make her worry a little more
As she'd be left alone in the silent hours she abhorred
Left alone to her thoughts
And all the memories of the past
Reminding of all that she had ever lost

26

Your Part in My Story

"**A**m I speaking to Aanya Ma'am?" said the person on the other side of the call.

"Yes"

"Ma'am I am speaking from Apollo Hospital, your reports have arrived and the doctor has advised you to visit the hospital at the earliest"

"Okay, thank you" this call triggered the flood of intimidating thoughts.

Ahh, I was dreading this news for days ever since my first visit to the gynaecologist in Gwalior and that is why I chose to avoid it as long as I could.

I took an appointment for that very evening when the reports arrived and I was intimated. I geared up all courage to walk myself into the hospital.

I have never liked hospitals; I would always pray not just for myself but everyone that no one should see a day when he has to visit a hospital but that's impractical and naïve right? The words like 'doctor', 'hospital', 'blood','operation', 'medical tests', 'surgery', 'ambulance' are sufficient to make my body numb. As a child I would start crying at the mere sight of blood, sometimes I would cry on getting hurt not because the injury caused pain and discomfort but because the sight of blood would make me cry.

I remember that day when I was in grade two and I just returned from school. The school bus would leave me on the road at the stop which was around two hundred meters from my house. I used to be excited to see my mother and would run my way home. That day I stumbled while running and got my knee injured, it was badly injured but right at that moment it only burnt and hurt a little. I got on my feet slowly and dusted myself. I had almost reached home and fell just about ten meters from the house door.

After a few seconds when I reached the door of the house and rang the doorbell the blood started oozing out of the scratched knee. My mother opened the door, my face was contorted as my eyes were squeezed a little and my nose wrinkled as if I was fighting something.

"How did you get hurt?" She asked with her gaze on my hurt knee.

I lowered my face and saw a lot of blood, the knee had turned red. That was it, I started wailing.

"I fell down… when I was running…. I wanted to come to you quickly" I managed to say while crying.

"My little girl" she hugged me

That is what mere sight of blood has always done to me. That was also the time when we as little kids in grade two would decide what we want to become in future. The teacher in moral science class would ask us different questions about us which one was this. All my friends would say that they wanted to be a doctor but I had blood phobia so I could not even copy their answer.

Life is cruel as I say and nothing else would suffice what I heard that day,

"Miss Aanya, cancer is found in both of your ovaries and has spread outside the pelvis to other parts of the abdomen; It is stage III of ovarian cancer," the doctor said as if reciting some specifications of a device before telling the customer that his device is now defective and explaining the defect. But how can I blame him too? It was after all something they did daily, a job very much like a shopkeeper.

"So how long before I die?" I too added as if asking how long would the device function?

"Well, hysterectomy and bilateral salpingo-oophorectomy (removal of both ovaries and fallopian tubes), debulking of as much of the tumour as possible, and sampling of lymph nodes and other tissues in the pelvis and abdomen that are suspected of harbouring cancer. After surgery, you may either receive combination chemotherapy possibly followed by additional surgery to find and remove any remaining cancer. The survival rate is 39% for five years in such cases. It depends on how you would respond to the treatment"

"Ahh, okay, well, hmm." I could not understand what else to say at that moment.

At least I did not start crying like a child before the doctor. He told me to make decisions quickly as every moment cancer would only spread to other organs.

Alas, the very ailment that feeds upon the spirits first and then the body.

I reached my apartment that night and was placid; there was a big question before me. Should I undergo all that pain and suffering of the horrific treatment, have my ovaries and fallopian tubes removed and then undergo chemotherapy just to see whether I live for another five years or not? Or should I just spend the rest of the time as a normal person does with a little fatigue and those symptoms which would slowly aggravate till my last breath is taken away?

Was there any point in going through those surgical and extreme medical procedures to extend my time by a couple of years? I was anyway going to live for a year or two without going through such torture to my body.

It was clear to me. The answer was obvious. I had made a choice.

Every individual has a story to recite as everyone's life is a story in itself. When we read history at school, we were introduced to history as 'his story' i.e. the story of man, so reading history was nothing but reading the stories of powerful and influential men of all times. Likewise, stories are always being written by people to be read by the coming generations.

I have always been keen to choose autobiographies over other genres of books because reading the life stories of real characters that existed has always been more intriguing for me. As I say each one of us has a story, some confine those stories to their heart, some read a few chapters aloud while some put their entire stories out. Each person's story too has many characters apart from him and those characters decide a substantial part of the plot. The role of the many characters cannot be overlooked at all.

When I think of how my story would be written and how your part in it would be described, I conclude that it would remain a mystery. I would never be able to decipher what purpose exactly you had to serve in my life, whether it was making me understand the meaning of love, the beauty of life, kindling the avariciousness for life, the joy of sharing oneself with someone or whether it was ultimately to lead me to an abysmal depth of despair where even the faintest ray of hope could not make its way.

I am but sure of the brevity of the part you played or rather the beautiful part you played because the happiness was succinct and lasted for a brief time.

But so did my life. The aftermath of your role has been devastating as you left me high and dry in the midst of chaos. Even in your absence, your memories do the job right. And now when I need you the most in the last days of my life, you are not here.

Whenever your character in my story would be expressed then it would be like a once in a lifetime moment that changes everything thereafter. That one huge transitional phase was brought about by one person. I am sure that I'm not just the only one who has experienced such drastic change in life by the arrival of a person; there are many others whose lives have been transformed for good or sometimes bad by just one person.

Romit, some goodbyes are so hard yet inevitable

This is how I would put it in words if asked to describe your part in my story,

Your part in my story
Remained a beautiful mystery
Brief and phenomenal

Alike that once in a lifetime moment
When the meteor showers blaze the sky
The gaze fixed at the marvellous sight
Which only left memories to recall
With a desire that it had been better my favourite song
In my playlist which I could play on and on
Rather than a meteor shower which couldn't be replayed
once gone
I was left stupefied
Like a child wondering about things mystified
With the blurry images with the passing time
Not even believing that it all happened as I read my
rhymes

27

A World of Fantasy

"Aanya what else can one desire for?" you asked with a grin on your face

"Nothing, I cannot be more blessed than being in the midst of nature, away from the hustle-bustle of human life," I said

I woke up this morning with the faint pictures from a dream I can see still fresh before my eyes. Have you ever noticed how these faint pictures from a dream just keep hovering in the mind all day and make us ruminate about it? I know I wouldn't even have shared this with you if you were here but since you are not, I am taking the liberty to write about it since it was the most beautiful one I have seen after a series of nightmares in real life.

It was just the two of us in some fantasy land where there was nothing like the societal norm. Things were normal and great as they were when we were together in college. We were in perfect health and spirit, full of life and so in love.

The land was abounding in nature and peace; there was the music of the rustling leaves and sometimes you could also feel the music of the wind, how it whispered in the ear as if carrying a message from some faraway land. It was just a manifestation of my heart's desires. There were only two of us in that landscape, no other human presence or none discernible.

On waking up I realize it was truly a fantasy, we cannot leave society and live somewhere on the island, it is not feasible. I dearly wish life could have been at least a little simple. This society is too complex, its ways do not serve the purpose of its creation which is human well being. On the contrary, it pushes a person to the edge, makes him take his own life. The societal pressure to meet the standards, excel, pretend to be happy in this rat race all adds up to devouring the spirits of a person. Is that why civilization came into being?

Simple things, modest lifestyles, unpretentious ways of life are not venerated anymore. The more complex anything can be, the more appreciated. A negligible fraction of the entire population on this planet understands that life is meant to be ordinary and simple.

My heart breaks on hearing of instances when little boys and girls who do not even reach the age of majority commit suicides because of the pressure to excel in academics, to clear competition exams and to win the race they didn't volunteer to run in. Imagine the extent of pressure on the young and naïve minds that taking their own lives seems easier to them rather than continue living in this suffocating environment of pressure.

I think a world where this pressure to conquer everything does not exist is also a fantasy. My own fantasy as it is my heartfelt desire but not possible. I wish there was a door that opened into such a plain world of fantasy.

They say dreams are the picturization of what hovers in the subconscious mind. You see how it is just you that I want along with me in a land where there is peace.

"Fantasy, this word always intrigued me Romit."

I could just never get how people had different fantasies. I believed everything was possible except for those alien and space fantasies which some had. So I always questioned why call it a fantasy if it is worldly possible? Just call it a goal or if it is remotely possible then call it a dream. I never had fantasies but today after that dream I realized what fantasy meant.

Fantasy is a heartfelt desire that is not possible. That dream is not possible and it is a fantasy.

I told you about the choice I made about my life in the last entry in my diary. I don't know after me if you would get this diary or not. It would be fortuitous if you do not because there is nothing written in it that would make you happy.

I know you still love me and it would be hard for you to love another woman that is why it is even more important that I burn this diary to ashes before becoming too weak to do that. I would want you to get along with life.

I have heard from our mutual friends that you are doing well in Canada. A couple of years would allow you to finally leave behind all that you had. And then if this news would break-in, you would handle yourself well.

Moving to Canada was never a part of your plan. When you did, I knew deep down that even you felt weak to face things living here. That must have been the reason that you moved and I understand this because even I did the same with the only difference that the country was the same.

I keep receiving calls from my parents about how I am doing and I have to lie to their faces. I do not want them to live in misery anticipating that their only daughter is going to leave them soon and never come back. I want them to live under ignorance because you know ignorance is bliss. That is not funny I know but ever since this ailment has been discovered I feel like finding humour in everything.

I have even come to peace with our separation, as it would have been unbearable for you to witness me pass away before your eyes. Everything thus happens for good, we just cannot see the good before.

If we keep this one faith that whatever happens, happens for good, something that we hear over a so many times in our lifetime but don't follow then so many complaints, resentment, pain, suffering would be eliminated from our lives. We will begin to notice the good in everything, even suffering can be turned into a great opportunity to realize the best. These words sound hollow during those moments when one goes through pain but once the dark clouds leave and the sky is clear and one looks back then it becomes clear why whatever happens, happens for good.

If a blessing is taken away, a greater blessing lies ahead. Trust the process.

I have bought a year from my parents before they force me to take saptapadi with someone else. I know that's the most I am going to live now and after a year there won't be another excuse needed.

The effect of the dream this morning was so strong that all day I couldn't help but only think about the possibility of the day when we could escape to another world of fantasy,

Let's just escape into a world of fantasy
And live the remaining of our lives with anonymity
For a moment close our eyes to imagine how it would feel
to be
There, in a whole new world with no check on our sanity
With unbridled love and joy, sharing affinity
For a moment just imagine despite it not being a
possibility
And gleam by the mere thought that, what if it could
actually be
A world of fantasy?

28

Drought of Words

Ever and anon on being asked how you are feeling, you are bereft of words if you honestly wish to describe how you feel because sometimes some feelings cannot be cribbed, caged and confined within words.

I have a lot of emotions mixed right now. Sometimes I feel grateful for having such a wonderful life though a little brief but I did all that I could and I found love, not many people do that. As for my parents, I was a good law-abiding daughter who made them proud by standing on her own feet. That is all I planned a few years ago, to finish graduation, stand on my feet, marry you, Romit and get actively involved in some community service which I have started now as time cannot wait any further.

It gives me a sense of wholeness again when I am able to help a cause and bring a smile to innocent faces. It makes me feel good, the moments I spend with the children in different NGOs trying to assist them with their studies and planting trees which I wanted to always do. I am grateful for all that.

I never wanted to start a family of my own as in having our own kids and you knew it too. So you did not even talk about it until I was willing to. I always had this idea that why to have a child only because he would carry our genes, there are so many children out here in the world who crave a family and the love they are deprived of. When we can be the ones taking the responsibility of one such child then why let go of this privilege.

I do not accept the absurd logic of the Indians behind having our biological kids, this is what I hear when it comes to this subject,

'Who will carry our generation further?

'There should be the same blood in the children's veins as ours'

'What? Should we give a message that we are biologically incapable of having kids?'

And many more which are enraging. This is only with respect to a gender-neutral kid. What is more absurd is wanting a son instead of a daughter because,

'One attains salvation only when one gives birth to a son'

'A daughter is a debt, can only bring dishonour to family'

'Our family's name can be carried on by a son only'

How ridiculous this can be, I wonder. You and I never gave in to the family pressure for having a child of our own. I am thankful that you were never of any such opinion.

There is a girl, Sarah who lives in Manav Kartavaya foundation's house for children. She is seven years old, very pretty like an angel but she has some trouble learning things easily and I am working on it. The first day when I met her, she sat quietly in a corner; she didn't seem to get along well with the other children. She was very quiet as if scared as if she did not receive the tenderness and love which one must at that age and before.

That was indeed true, she was left at an orphanage at the age of three, Manav Kartavaya brought her to the house last year itself. She did not receive what a child is rightful ought to. There is something that draws me towards her more than any other child.

The reason I am telling you is that if by chance I miss to burn this diary or dispose of it and you happen to read it then maybe meet her. If we were together and I had more years to live, I would have brought her home. I see so much of myself in her, the quite shy girl. My eyes become moist at times when she is before me as my desire to bring her up is nothing more than a fantasy now.

Those moments I tell you to make me forget what I am battling inside. I don't remember any of my own life and rejoice in the innocence and happiness of those children. That is exactly how I would have loved to spend my last days here on this planet, amid happiness and innocence. That's where we complete each other, I crave for love which they give me and in turn, they get the love they crave for.

This is a lot better than having my body parts removed surgically and spending days in the hospital or the bed with a heavy dose of medicines. Who would want to die with that? Though I am taking some prescriptions for minimizing the symptoms and maintaining little health how long before that keeps me going? The disease will soon spread to the vital organs and that's when nothing would work.

There are also some days when I just don't wish to step out; I don't wish to see the sun and I keep myself confined to my room alone. I don't exactly know how I feel, numb, vulnerable, weak or depressed. Not a single word describes it right. I feel lost or in a state of hysteria. I strongly feel that I need help but I don't find words to describe how I would put my dilemma before someone else. There has never before been a drought of words in my life, these words were my only aid to describe everything that I felt. And today,

I don't have words, how do I describe
It's like a drought of words, to suffice
Don't even understand how to put it right
Maybe I'm just scared and trapped inside
Afraid to go out and face the sun
It feels cosy inside with darkness and no one
I might spend a few more days without the sun
And survive indoors with a little halogen
Might end up reading the whole dictionary
With a hope something would describe the feeling that is
so eerie

29

And What Not?

I can recall that city bus travels in Delhi during my college years and also the Haryana and Rajasthan roadways by which I would commute sometimes to see my friend Rita in Jaipur. Those pamphlets stuck next to the windows in the bus always caught my attention because I found them amusing.

'For marriage, foreign travel, finding lost love, money, property etc contact Baba XYZ, Contact number- …'

This Baba could solve all the human predicaments. And I wondered who those people to contact him were. I understand the predicament of the troubled souls now.

When we get tired of enduring things, we decide to look for remedies that can cure us of our malady or if not cure then at least dwindle the intensity of the pain it inflicts. After reaching the zenith of our capacity to endure we even don't care what remedies are offered to us, we just want to get rid of the pain at any cost. This is like visiting a doctor with the words in the mouth, "Cure me, I don't care how, I just want to recover" or making prayers to god, even to those in whose existence you didn't believe before. Isn't that true, Romit?

We become desperate to do away with the pain we have been enduring for a long. I have seen people who resort to drugs, alcohol and any stupefying or intoxicating things at their disposal just to do away with the mental suffering. It is more like a diversion or distraction from their miseries. Several artists take birth out of the jarring trial of life, for them, art is the distraction.

In the course of twenty-six years of my life or if I say all of my life, I have come across many kinds of people, witnessed people in pain, seen them undergo transformation after some life turning point. If I were to live longer I might have seen many more kinds but even to this date, I can safely conclude that irrespective of where we come from, what we do our status or anything that we identify ourselves with, irrespective of all this we behave in the same manner in the face of enduring adversity persistently. We all become desperate to get rid of the pain.

In India, there are so many people who make money at the expense of someone's misery. This is facilitated by the fact that people are also superstitious and tend to believe anything which a rational mind would not. So many scams take place every day in the name of curing ailments by supernatural means.

This holds true for at least Hindus in India. I belong to a Hindu family and thus I have witnessed so many superstitions being so strongly and blindly followed by my parents and relatives that the fear has been instilled in my own mind.

"Romit, let's wait for someone else to pass"

I said once when we were both walking past the circle of our department building in campus. We both saw the cat cross our path. I had always been told that a cat crossing your path brings bad luck or misfortune. So many times it was told with a firm conviction that even I unconsciously started fearing what if it does, so I would better wait for someone else to cross the path.

"Are you serious Aanya?" you said ridiculing as you read my thoughts.

"These are all superstitions; you are a rational person then how could you believe these?"

And then while we were talking someone else walked past the path and I was relieved.

"Yeah, let's go. No problem" I said.

This is just one such instance which we shared. There are innumerable superstitions that exist in India. The more diverse the population the more diverse we see the superstitions. Number 13 being unlucky, keeping a knife under the pillow to drive away nightmares, eye twitching where one eye brings luck and the other misfortune, crow shits on you and you are going to be lucky, warding off evil with lemon and chillies, eating curd before going to work, cutting hair and nails on Thursday, Saturday and after sunset brings bad luck, itchy palms signify good fortune or marks the arrival of money and so many more. These are the ones which I have been led to believe by my parents as they would not let me do a thing that brings bad luck.

Apart from the superstitions, the remedies which are at an Indian's disposal are vast in number. From astrology to religion to tantra/black magic to whatnot, the preachers are ready to offer you a solution for every problem. You can do anything by merely wearing a stone or paying a visit to any temple or shrine or conducting some religious practice and whatnot. And when we become desperate then we let go off all the logic and reasoning and just give in to what they say.

Emotional pain can also be so exhausting and we need to deal with it before it devours our spirit completely. Sincerely speaking writing every day to you lessens my misery. I now believe how keeping a journal can be effective in dealing with emotional havoc. This is one of the few things that have worked out for me.

I wouldn't be exaggerating when I say that even I resorted to everything possible to somehow get along with life. I tried things that never in the past made any sense to me because even I had lost the capacity to endure more. Today it just,

Feels like an era has just passed
Yet there's no replacement to what I had lost
Knocked the doors of the ones who provide different ointments
Drank elixir, the alleged cure to all ailments
Kneeled at sacred places of different religions and faith
Praying and invoking the superior beings
With a hope, I'll be cured by something at least
Paid heed to the prophets and the crystal gazers
Been with the gypsies for some favours
There's wasn't any stone left unturned
Yet the malady went growing within
Seemed like to cure this, there wasn't a thing
In the face of sheer darkness
I had lost the ability to see the silver lining

30

Can We Be?

"We have thought to pay you a visit, it has been a few months since you moved to Ahmedabad" My mother said on the phone.

"Why do you want to take the trouble? I am doing fine"

"It is no trouble to come and see our only daughter, we shall visit you next week" and she hung up.

This was not the maiden effort when this idea was proposed by my mother; she had constantly been catechizing the same since the day I moved here. She also proposed if they could drop me off but I kept shunning any such thing. I needed space to grapple with my condition. I did not even meet any friend of ours Romit. Maybe I have become a little selfish to have the little time left all to myself and to you.

There are these thoughts that have been hovering in my mind since she called,

"Will they be able to tell that I am sick?"

"Is it just enough to hide the truth from my parents?"

No, it isn't. They are my parents after all and they deserve to know about it. But then what would that lead to?

Only pain and suffering, they wouldn't be able to stop the inevitable so isn't it better than they are spared of the mental agony too.

Ovarian cancer has so vague symptoms that it goes unnoticed for years; in my case too it went unnoticed for a long time before it spread to the adjoining organs. After all, who can think of it when one experiences something, almost all the people do today like loss of weight, appetite, bloating etc. it has become normal with the lifestyle that we follow these days.

Even till recently the symptoms were all vague and had it not been my father's insistence I would not even have bothered to get it checked. Now it is too late and with survival chances of 39% I was not going to get my body parts removed and live the rest of my few years with an operated body lacking some of its vital organs.

So be it. Let me live the last few months I have happily, doing my community service as long as the body allows and not let anyone suffer from the fact that I am a guest for some months now.

"I feel I am not doing justice to my parents and not even you, Romit." But this is for everyone's best, we can't stop the unavoidable so why grieve over it.

We by and large have no idea about what someone must be going through in his life at any point intime. Like no one knows about what I am going through at this point. If some stranger would be a little rude to me then I certainly would weep back home.

A simple smile or gesture of kindness can make one's day, maybe that may turn out to be the only good thing that happens to him the entire day. I have always believed that being kind and having compassion for fellow beings is inherent to being a human yet I'm taken aback at how people today deal with other human being.

It's the basic, surprising acts of generosity that change lives, and a zenith of these little acts can change the world, make it a better place to be. We should search for the positive qualities in others, and when we discover it, how about we treat them like that is all we see.

We don't need to anticipate that anything consequently all together should be caring. With generosity, the provider benefits similarly so much, if not more, than the receiver of those acts. How about we make it our objective to make at any rate one individual's day, consistently, and perceive how our own lives are changed all the while. Given the circumstances, we're all in this together.

A troubled mind finds stability and peace by doing some simple acts of kindness; it makes us feel more positive towards life. I speak of my own experience.

"Is everything okay now?" I asked the watchman of the society I lived in.

"Yes Madam, you are nice," he said with a heart-warming smile on his face.

He was having a bad day since morning; a stray dog entered the society campus and sat on the top of Mr Ahuja's car. Mr Ahuja lives in the same building where I do. When in the morning he reached the parking space and found it sitting on the top, he screamed at the top of his voice hurling abuses at the watchman. Our watchman is a dutiful person who does not usually waive off his duties.

"This is what you are paid for? To snore during duty while any stray animal comes in?" Mr Ahuja yelled

"Sorry Sir, I don't know when it sneaked inside" his voice was shaky.

The poor watchman had to face his wrath. He greets me cheerfully every time I pass by the main entrance but today evening, he sat with a long face. I asked him and he narrated the incident. I also learnt that he was upset over the failing health of his mother; she was too sick these days. He seemed a little lost for that reason.

What did I do that brought a smile on his face? Well I brought some bottle gourd juice on my way back, bottle gourd you know relieves bloating and indigestion; I asked him that he must have it with me because I did not have any friends around and it felt too miserable. It was a little effortful to convince him. Meanwhile having juice together I also said,

"I don't like Mr Ahuja, grumpy man, have you noticed his nose moves when he yells" and that's when he smiled, almost laughed.

At whatever point we carry out something beneficial for an individual, the staggering sensation of bliss is inescapable. We feel great since we are the explanation for somebody's smile. This chain response makes us more joyful and more satisfied.

Just be kind
There's suffering all around
People going through trying times
It's heart breaking to see mankind
Ignoring things as if blind
Why can't there be empathy
And hearts with some sympathy
Everyone goes through ordeals
And needs some love to heal

Can't we all promise this time
To be each other's solace
As it's a long hard climb?

31

Parched

There are times in our life when we have to fight our own battles by our bootstraps. Despite having people around there are times when you have to go through the ordeal un-aided. How does it feel then putting up with all the setbacks that life has designed exclusively for you?

Some Gordian knots are solely for you. The pain cannot be allayed by anyone even if they are ready to.

My parents stayed here for two days. They were pleased to meet the little kids I taught together with Sarah at the NGOs and I showed them the little saplings that we planted in the city. All these events evinced cheerfulness on their long faces.

I particularly took care that they interact with Sarah, get to know her and have her picture saved in their memory.

"This is my favourite girl, Sarah," I said beaming with joy as if I introduced my own child.

"Hello dear, how are you?" my mother asked with the tenderness that mothers display with children

"Does Aanya Ma'am help you in learning?" my father asked her as if humorously inquiring about how well I was doing my duty.

Sarah stayed quiet and sheepishly came around behind me, she held me as if saying that she wasn't comfortable with new people. Yes, she wasn't, it took over a week to metamorphose from a stranger to be kept at a distance to her friend she could trust and get her talking freely with me. One thing which I believe was serendipitous about my parents' visit was that they met Sarah.

I longed for your presence too Romit, if something could just get you to India till I am still here and I could see you meet her, little angel.

They believed that I was getting along with life and will be ready to start a new life with someone new soon. However, the truth wasn't what they perceived.

For those two days, I felt more lonesome as I had to pretend that things were great. On the outside, my body looked weaker but I led them to believe that it was the work and then community service and this new city and food. They bought it too as this could be the reason make one lose some health.

"There is this guy, Sunny" my mother initiated something I avoided all this while on the telephonic conversations we had. During one of the evenings when we sat together in Ahmedabad in my apartment, she with a firm face brought the conversation here.

We three sat in the drawing-room which was comfortably large to accommodate a sofa set. The apartment was meant for one person only; there was a room, a small drawing-room, a bathroom, kitchen and balcony.

"Ohh yes, there are a lot of guys on this planet, I know," I said trying to end this here with a wisecrack but of no avail.

"We met him during your cousin's wedding we attended last month, we told you to come but you were so occupied with work" she went on ignoring what I had just said and giving the impression that she would not stop until she finishes no matter what I say.

"He is a genteel man, twenty-nine, runs his family business which is impressive. He is refined" she said as if trying to sell her product to me.

"Hmm, that is good," I said expressing disinterest which my parents could clearly discern.

"So we want you to meet him soon before he finds another match" she looked distressed and pronounced this last statement.

"You should get along with life, such opportunities do not knock on the door often" my father supported.

"Okay, just a few months more? I have just started getting back on feet" I said knowing that this they might consider over a straight no.

And they did. They left filled with rosiness for me and my future. I feel that the impetus behind their visit was to convince me of this proposal. I am not being cynical; it is after all they reckon to be for my best interests.

After all, one cannot spend an entire lifetime alone, one needs companionship. It is good to have a person who is with you in both the highs and lows throughout your life. I would not be happy to see any Sharma Uncles around, forlorn and arousing sympathy.

They were concerned about my life, little did they know I didn't have to spend a life all alone, it was a few days more or maybe months.

This made me bawl the night they left. I was battling all this alone and I felt guilty, so guilty for giving false hopes to my parents who I loved so much. It hurt me more than I anticipated. I slept like a new-born curled up like a ball.

A taste of how it feels
Being parched, all alone
Underneath the scorching sun's heat
With the ruthless Sirocco trying to beat
In a fight indicating dead heat
Draining out all the energy
Much alike a fish out of water
Restless, trying to fight and succeed
Taking all directions
Leading to mirage, just another deceit
Losing all hopes for life
Reminiscing memories bitter and sweet
Much alike a fish out of water
Knowing this picture to be a slaughter
That's how it feels

32

Wish to Be Read

"I will get it, Didi," my maid said while I tried to get out of bed.

"You know what I want?" I inquired

"Water? You get up only for two things either to use the restroom or get water" she asked seeking confirmation

"You have begun to know me so well; yes I want some water, lukewarm." I said relieved, she noticed everything, even the frequent visits to the toilet.

"You are becoming weak day by day, why don't you ask a doctor?" she looked concerned.

"Nothing to worry about, the doctor has said it shall pass," I told her trying to calm her.

"Okay if you say so"

Seema has been working fora few days, now that my body has lost the strength to manage both the household chores and work, I hired her. She comes every morning and finishes major work and then leaves in the afternoon, later she comes again in the evening and willingly stays till I retire to bed. She lives not very far from our society, just a ten-minute walk to reach home. She is married and her husband works at an automobile repair shop.

I like her presence in the apartment as she gets everything, I don't speak out loud, she quite understands me.

The desire to be understood is one of the abecedarian needs of a human being. One wants to be understood, accepted and loved and there is no greater gratification than the one which he gets on being understood, accepted and loved.

Can you recall Romit, once you asked me?

"What do you want me to change about myself Aanya?"

"Why would you want to change anything about yourself?"

"No, I mean if there's something that you don't like about me, I would change it"

"Well, when I said that I loved you, it meant 'you' and you are everything that makes 'you'. How can I then ask to let go of anything that makes you 'you'? And if I would ask then I don't think that would still be called love. I have accepted you in your entirety and I am no one to tell you to change yourself for anyone"

"I love you so much Aanya"

You felt loved and I hope I made you feel that you belonged with me. That is what everyone wants right? Acceptance and understanding

We find comfort in the company of people who think the way we do because that is when they understand us and also accept us the way we are. The old saying which goes, 'birds of the same feather flock together' somewhere finds its sole basis on the same fact.

Many relations turn fragile because one person is not understood by the other. This lack of understanding makes the strongest of relations between people collapse. Even the parent-child relation, the strongest amongst all does not sustain due to lack of understanding.

Understanding, acceptance and tolerance is the way of life and that is what Hinduism is. Today when I see people defying the basic idea on which lays the foundation of Hinduism, it aches. I see riots, disharmony and conflicts in the society for some differences that exist between them in terms of gender, caste, religion etc. Who has taught these trouble makers such non-acceptance and intolerance I wonder? No religion surely does.

"Romit, you must be wondering how even while dying I would not stop criticizing"

I just can't. I feel sadder at how the world is plagued today with so many problems all of which are man-made. The advent of civilizations was to serve the human purpose of existing peacefully and in harmony with each other and nature. Today however it has served a contradictory role, we were better hunters and wanderers then I suppose at least nature was unharmed. Now life's existence on Earth is itself in danger because of humans. How to turn a blind eye to these facets while dying? I become more attentive instead. What future does the coming generation have?

I hope you would understand my mental state as I went from the desire of being understood to some worldwide issues, Romit. You must be wondering if this is a diary or some elongated article on human society. Well, consider it both, as this is all that will be left of me after I am gone.

At this moment I wish to be understood by you and the people around me who don't see the ordeal I am going through but they perceptibly cannot without being aware of the real state of facts.

You never really understood me which turned out to be the reason behind our downfall despite the love that was the binding force.

"I don't understand you"

You said after three years of being with me without understanding the nature of damage these words could cause.

"You change with time; you adopt very soon or I do not know what it is but I don't think that I understand you Aanya" was your added explanation.

I went on to think if it was me who changed over the years or was it you who could not understand me and found an excuse.

Did I expect a lot in wanting my partner to understand me? This was another question I had at that time.

"Maybe you are right, I am not the same person and I evolve with time," I said swallowing all the soreness that your words caused.

All the years I only wished to be understood by you. Unfortunately, very few are blessed with a partner who understands them fully. If I would have had the chance to tell you just how much I wanted to be understood this is how I would have put it,

> *I wish to be read*
> *Alike the way I read my favourite books*
> *Wish all my emotions to be deciphered in a look*

Which are hidden and remain unexpressed
Alike the way I understand the emotions repressed
Of the author who expresses those in disguise
I wish your eyes to get stuck at me with surprise
Just the way mine are glued to its pages
I wish that you understand me without me having to
beseech
Just the way I understand all the figures of speech
How I wish for you to look into my eyes
And visualize the dreams that we would soon actualize
Just the way I always like to travel
Into the imagination of the writer

33

Breaking

At some point in life, we all feel like we are breaking mostly at times when we no longer can bear the pain.

"Maybe we should get separated before more damage is done to this relation," you said not even looking into my eyes

My mind was already clogged on hearing these words; somewhere I felt this wasn't possible at all. In the fury and heat that was there because of these words, I too said,

"Do what you feel is right!"

I did not know that was it. The end! Arguments and exchange of bitter words between the people who love each other is not unusual. It is the wrath that makes us spill harsh words, deep down there is only love. I mistakenly thought that fight to be one of the ordinary ones.

One heated conversation and everything would end, I never thought. It did not end right then, of course, it was the beginning of the end. Having such conversations became the order of the day. Long unbroken silences would sometimes last for days. The beautiful phase of life ended with the heated conversation we had that day. The stars began to do their work and we parted our ways gradually which finally ended with our divorce.

I wonder if that day you had not proposed the idea of separation or I had not reacted to it that way then could things have been any different?

Today, it makes no sense if things could have gone differently or not, today I feel it was for the best.

It has been five months since my parents visited Ahmedabad, since I gave them my word to meet the guy they liked. The symptoms of the ailment have aggravated that I no longer go to work.

"Your health had been deteriorating since you joined; you were mostly on leave during the last month. Is there anything you have been keeping from us?" my supervisor asked when I resigned.

"No sir, I think the place did not suit me. I would leave this place soon" me telling the truth as I was going to leave soon.

"You have been an asset to us and I wish you luck for your future endeavours," he said goodbye.

"Thank you, Sir" I left.

I had been saving a major chunk of my monthly salaries first because I had nothing to spend on and second because I knew I would need it for my last days.

I consulted another doctor just to know precisely how much time I had. I had one month more. I was not living like any other cancer patient with all the side effects of the treatment. In my case, I only had to deal with the failing of the organs. I developed quite a relationship with my toilet, to be honest, ha-ha. Most of the days I would ask Seema to cook porridge or just boiled vegetable soup. The picture was getting grim.

I took medicines to minimize the symptoms as far as possible. To some extent, those helped in relieving some pain.

I yearned for spending these last days with my parents, with you, with my friends. I had not seen anyone in the past five months. But I knew my spirits might break if I had anyone before me.

Perhaps what I would even say Romit?

This is not my favourite movie or novel when some abracadabra mantra is spelt out in the end and everything that was lousy rolls over to being good again. This is not fiction but life and life is real. There is no witchcraft here and the inevitable happens eventually. There is no magic wand to turn around events.

This is no fairy tale to always have a happy end and we must acknowledge that. I wish I could write my own story and give it a happy ending with a sudden twist of events just the way it happens in movies.

When I think of all of you, I feel that no justification would ever validate the betrayal. So I have killed the instinct to be with my people in my last days. I have recorded some videos for my parents and family explaining that I wanted myself and everyone else to live contentedly for as long as I had time. A little explanation might act as an ointment.

Some videos were of me with the kids I taught which captured the happiest moments I had after coming to Ahmedabad. This would lessen the agony of my parents I thought when they would know that I was happy during all this time.

I felt that recurring melancholy every night in the dead and silent hours when a string of pernicious thoughts would cross my mind. Haven't you ever told yourself that let this be the end, there is no wish to continue any longer?

I would tell that to myself every night believing that I have lost the capacity to endure. The next morning life would again demand strength to live for some more days and I would listlessly continue to go on. The fall of the day would again inflict excruciating misery which would make me want to give up.

Sometimes to feel better and avoid the anxiety, I would take walk on the terrace and keep walking to and fro until I get some air to make me feel better again. I have lived on the edge of survival and reached the breaking point.

Hope has been my only aid to help me survive the darkest of days. Hope that you are doing fine and would do great in the time to come. Hope that I did the right thing by saving everyone I loved from the pain they would have had to go through if they knew.

I was walking to and fro
As the pain couldn't let me settle, it continued to grow
Saying it was excruciating was no exaggeration
It was testing me and my determination
I couldn't really understand
This time why I couldn't even withstand
I wished to whimper
But couldn't do that, a thing so simple
I had been fighting it for hours and did not even weep

My eyes weighed heavy in need of sleep
But there seemed no end
I was breaking, I couldn't pretend

34

Just a Moment

The beauty of life is in the uncertainty of just anything and everything. Every new day is a surprise and every next moment is unforeseeable. We never know what is to come next; life is unpredictable at its best.

Now just imagine watching a thriller movie which you have already watched in the past? Is it as breathtaking like it was when you watched it for the first time? No, not because you know how the story would unfold.

Would you participate in any event already knowing the outcome of it? Or even if you do would you have the same enthusiasm and spirit? The same thing is indubitable when it comes to life, if you already know what is to happen next then you will be reduced to a lifeless being with no avariciousness for life. It is only enticing to know about the future when you know that you cannot.

So it is better to embrace this beauty of uncertainty. It takes just a moment for things to go wrong or right, just a moment for any catastrophe to destroy the planet, just one moment for anyone to cease breathing and everything else happens in a moment.

We should accept the impermanence of everything. Trying to hold on to what has to pass only adds to suffering.

I have made peace with my short journey.

Even I have accepted that our lovely brisk expedition was no exception to this rule. It was also impermanent and was destined to end either sooner or later. We do not anticipate some things to end soon and when those things finally bite the dust, we are left broken but accepting the truth of this universe aids in abating the melancholy.

This might be the last page that I am writing as I have a couple of days more before this ordeal finally settles. I don't know what the next moment holds, maybe if this is the last one, I have? There is something I want to write over and over again as I would not get a chance again.

"You made me appreciate life Romit, made me feel the depth and intensity of every emotion. You made me a better person and you were the only one I loved more than myself and I am sorry"

People who fall in love become better persons and I am no exception. They become sensitive to life; they understand human emotions better. We learn to live in the present when we are in love.

However as a run of the mill being our importunity is after knowing what the future holds for us, it is not uncommon to see people calling on astrologers, reading horoscopes and doing anything told to them just to get a hint of what the future holds for them. Well in my case all it took was an appointment with the doctor to know what the future holds for me. Humorous, isn't it Romit?

But have we ever cared to wonder that we would be destroying the very beauty of life by knowing what the next moment is to bring about in your life? I don't mean stop visiting doctors and get treated. It's about other subtle aspects of life. Let's just live in the present, in the moment.

This applies very much to people who want to forever cling to their past. So this is especially for you, I hope you would let go off your past and live in the moment.

I hope that you find love again, I sincerely do. Though it may not be the same as it was before, maybe you wouldn't feel the butterflies you felt earlier, maybe you wouldn't do stupid things in love, maybe your heart won't throb at your love's sight like it used to, maybe love will be a little mature this time but it will be love.

Who says we can't love someone else after having loved someone before? Was love given to you in short supply that you finished it all over one person? The ways might change but love always remains. Everyone rants they can't find love again? Why even narrow down the definition of love to just feeling it for your lover? Don't we love our family, friends even our pet or anything else? It's time we realize that as humans love is our nature, we must relish in this beautiful emotion before it gets too late.

I regret having lamented over the last year because I too believed what most people do, the realization dawned upon me too late but when it did, I began to observe how beautiful life is and how one can enjoy even the most ordinary things in life. I hope that you do not make the same mistake I did. Romit lives when you still have time.

> *So how is it that in a moment the world turns upside down,*
> *One can go about from playing a king to a clown*

Just a fraction of second is what it takes
To lose or win anything you had put at stake
Awe-inspiring is this play that life has staged
Everyone playing a part, that's what has always prevailed
Transient is everything that exists, I say
Just as illusion, to deceive you anyway
So, a moment is what it takes
To lose it all despite no mistakes

Epilogue

Aanya called her friend Rita a night before her last entry in the diary. She explained her all that had been going on all this time and told her to come to her without telling anyone else about it. Rita knew Aanya from college and was also Romit's friend. She did not keep quiet and told Aanya's parents about her condition.

Aanya's parents arrived the next day when Rita did. They did not express resentment on being kept in the dark but wanted to love their daughter as much as they could for how much time was left. Aanya was admitted to the hospital given her condition and she passed away a week later.

The recorded videos were the last of what she left for her parents. Her parents grieved like any other parent would have on the demise of their only child. However in one of the videos with the kids at the NGO, she was with Sarah and said,

"Consider her your Aanya and don't feel that I have left"

Aanya's parents adopted Sarah and saw their daughter's reflection in her. Finally, someone was there to fill the void that Aanya had created by her absence. Romit was not told anything until Aanya was no longer with them. He arrived in India on getting the unfortunate news that shook him to the core. He didn't look fine.

On being told about Sarah he told Aanya's parents,

"I would be her guardian too, she might need the love that you two can give her but in future, she would need someone after you, I would take her responsibility."

He kept making visits to India often because of Sarah. He did not marry again in his life. What about the dairy? Aanya told Rita to give away all her books to the NGO and the diary went away with it. Don't know if out there someone is reading her story but she saved Romit of the pain.

And as they say, life goes on.

About the Author

I struggled in expressing myself all my life until I took to writing in the latter years of my college. It turned out to be the most suitable way for me to express anything I wanted. The journey began from writing entries on random days in a diary to writing poems and then finally this book. Writing has almost become a part of me now.

I am a lawyer and a yoga practitioner. I am a poet and a writer too, my journey as an author began when I compiled a collection of my poems and published it in the year 2019 under the title, 'Dazzled by Illusion' and then another similar collection under the title 'Gray Pages' in 2020. I like to explore all that I can in life, this moment is all that is and living it to the fullest is what life is all about.

I graduated in the year 2020 in BA LLB from Amity University Rajasthan as a gold medallist and am pursuing my Masters in Law from MNLU. Writing and becoming an author was not in the plan but life is what happens to us while we are busy making our plans. And I feel complete when I write and I am grateful that at some point in life I started writing.